LOVE IN THE LYRICS

FALLING FOR A MUSIC MOGUL

ANNITIA L. JACKSON

ACKNOWLEDGMENTS

This book is intended to entertain and is recommended for ages eighteen and up. This is a book based on urban fiction, which consists of violence, offensive language, and sexual content.

I would like to dedicate this book to my grandmother, Hattie Fletcher. She is my guardian angel in heaven. She taught me to follow my dreams. I will always be indebted to her for that. Love you, Mama!

I just want to take this time to say thanks to my husband, Ron Jackson, for encouraging me and having my back while I took a step out on faith. Thank you for being an amazing father to our son, Nathan, and keeping his eight-year-old energy at bay while I write. You are my soul mate and helped me to understand what real love is. Thank you for being understanding when I have to write, and you say, "Baby, I got this. You just go do what you need to do." I love you and Nathan to the moon and beyond.

I want to also thank my middle school teacher, Barbara Middlebrooks, for introducing me to writing. You woke up a fire in me that I never knew existed. To my personal reading crew, Zeanola, Shawauna, Sharene, Brittany, HuAnna, Tina, Teamkia, Tanessia, Mickaya, Rachel, Lisa, Sweets, Stacey, and Kristi, that will share their opinions both good and bad, I want to thank you for helping me. I love you ladies so much!! I would also like to thank my sister, Kasandra, my cousin, Ingrid, and my nephew, Robert. Also, I would like to thank my aunt Gale for her spiritual guidance. You guys are my inspiration for going after my dream of being an author. I have watched you all accomplish your goals and it inspired me. And to my riders who always have my back, Renee, and Freda, I love you both so much.

I also want to thank the ladies in Bookies for taking a chance on my book and helping get the word out about it! Love you, admins!!!

Zee, I have so much love and respect for you and all you do. You are amazing, and you have been a true blessing to me. I always tell people how much you mean to me and the other authors you help. Continue, to do your thing because you are a true Queen.

My Law! I love you to death because you always give me honest and real conversation. You are one of the first people I see in my inbox in the morning, and I know that my mood, if bad, will be lifted. We started out with tacos and time zones and ended up as friends. Thank you for reading my work and keeping me laughing.

To Latoya Nicole Williams, my AG, thank you for being an

inspiration as an author, mother, and friend. I love you to pieces and back.

LIT-erary Queens!! You ladies are the real MVP's! You ladies are very important to me, I value your opinions and comments because they have really helped me grow as an author. Each one of you have helped me and I can't thank you enough.

Thank you, Assembly Literary Services, for making my book shine, by editing and helping me improve my craft. You are the bomb Franny!

Also, a big thanks to my promoters who work their asses off making sure everyone knows about my books! Vaneka Miles, who has been going hard from me since the beginning! My sis Alexis Crystal who goes hard for each one of my books! Also, Zee Fryer and Margaret Cooper who flood those groups daily! You all are the bomb and I appreciate you all so much!

Big thanks to my sis Iesha Bree, who makes most of my covers and does all of my typesetting and formatting! Thank you for my cover addiction, LOLOL!

To my writing boo, Latisha Smith Burns, thank you so much for being a listening ear and shoulder to cry on!!! You are awesome, and I don't know what I would do without you!

I would like to thank God for blessing me with the opportunity to do something that I love to do. Because without Him, I wouldn't be here today or have the storytelling gift that He blessed me with.

To my readers... words cannot express what you mean to me. Thank you for reading my work and giving me critiques to help me better my craft. I

am always available to hear your comments and opinions. I love you, ALJ readers!!!!

Love in the Lyrics: Falling for a Music Mogul

Synopsis:

Elle Jamison is engaged to popular R&B singer GT Wells. The pair fell in love and vowed to be there for each other no matter what. So, when an opportunity arose, Elle put her dreams of becoming a singer on hold, while GT pursued his dreams. She thought they were well on their way to starting their lives together until the fame went to his head. What started off as a fairy tale is now a nightmare filled with paternity tests, groupies, and disrespect. She wants to break free but feels she has no way out. Will she change her mind before her wedding date approaches?

Music mogul Savior Morrison is one of the top producers and songwriters in the music industry. After losing his wife and child a few years ago, he has sworn off finding love and having a family of his own. He pours himself into his work and changes women like he changes his underwear. Savior has no plans to change his ways or open his heart up ever again. That is until a melodic beauty's voice brings not only his lyrics to life, but his battered heart as well.

As all great love songs go, the road to love is filled with drama, betrayal, and enemies at every turn. Will these two find love in the lyrics or will their love fall flat?

PROLOGUE

Savior

POP! POP! POP!

"Savior! Help me!" Lake cried out to me as the bullets hit our bodies, knocking us both off our feet.

I watched as my wife lay on the ground, dying as I fought through my own pain to get to her. Every time I tried to crawl toward her, the distance between us kept growing. Her eyes were wide open and vacantly staring into the sky and blood leaked from her closed mouth, which made me frown because I kept hearing her voice begging for help.

"Lake, I'm coming, baby, hang on!"

"It's too late, you didn't save us! We're dead because of you! I begged you to change your life for us, but you waited and look what happened! I hate you, Savior!" Lake's voice echoed in my head over and over again. *"I hate you! I hate you! You killed us!*

"Lake!" I screamed as I sat up.

My body was covered in sweat as I looked around and realized I was in my bed at home. The nightmares the past few weeks had gotten worse, and it was because of Lake's impending birthday.

It had been two years since she was murdered and the pain of losing her never got easier. The memories of her only seemed to get stronger around her birthday, which triggered these nightmares and feelings of guilt more.

Most of the time when I got this way, I would bury myself in work or partying. Barely eating or sleeping to escape the agony of losing the love of my life. My brother and his wife were always telling me that Lake would want me to move on and be happy, but how could she want me to be happy when I was the cause of her and our child's death?

The decision to be alone and remain that way was my punishment for my part in their deaths. I dibbled and dabbled to take care of my physical needs, but that was as far as I was allowing myself to go. I had my chance at having a wife and children, but I fucked it up by being selfish and greedy. Happily ever after was not in the cards for me.

I felt myself getting sleepy, but I knew what was waiting for me as soon as I closed my eyes--Lake's ghost. Climbing out of my bed, I took a shower, threw on some clothes, and headed to the one place I could escape, the studio.

"ELLE, YOU KNOW GT IS NOT GOING TO WANT YOU IN THAT plain ass dress for the wedding! It's too damn sexy and looks like a nightgown! Plus, it's white. GT specifically said he wants you both in ivory because white doesn't look good on him and everyone does white. You have to remember this wedding is being shopped around for a reality show and some of the top entertainment magazines in the world. Your mama and I agreed that you should wear an ivory ballgown by Pnina Tornei. We have already contacted her, and she will be here next week for a consultation. Of course, she is charging GT big time because the wedding is only a few months away, but this wedding has to be top shelf!" Brooke insisted.

My heart sank as I looked at the beautiful Grecian style white wedding gown, draped and hugging my body like it was made for it. I didn't want a big sparkly ass wedding dress or this circus of a wedding, I had been told we were having. I had no choice in the matter just like everything else in my life. My life had become what was good for GT's image and lifestyle. This should have been the happiest time in my life right now--shopping for my wedding dress--but instead, I was being told what to wear to my own wedding.

"Brooke, I have gone along with everything you and my mother have come up with for this wedding, but this gown is more my personality. This is what I want to get married in, not a huge rhinestone-encrusted ball gown."

"Fine, Elle, if that's what you want then you are the bride. But before we place the order, let me send this pic to GT, so he can see what you are ordering," she replied as her fingers went to work on her phone.

My phone instantly rang, and I knew exactly who it was before I even looked at the screen. I took a deep breath and prepared for the bullshit I was about to hear.

"Hey, Grant. How are things going in the studio?"

"I told you stop calling me Grant! My name is GT now, Elle. Look, you can't wear that cheap shit to our fucking wedding! We are going to be making a lot of money off these wedding pictures and nobody wants to see your plain-looking ass in a two-thousand-dollar dress, when your man is worth millions. Now, Brooke showed me the pictures from the designer her and your mama picked, and that's who's making your dress. It needs to have so much fucking bling on it that a mutherfucker can see his reflection when you walk down the aisle. People need to see that I drop bags on my woman because I can afford it. Also, why does your damn hair look like you didn't comb that shit this morning! That's why they keep dogging your ass out on social media," Grant demanded.

I looked over and saw Brooke smirking and wanted to beat her fucking ass. She lived to snitch on me and cause problems in her brother's and my relationship. It was fucked up because she was supposed to be my best friend. As usual, no one was in my corner, not even my own damn mama. As long as she was on the GT gravy train, his opinion was the only one that mattered. The people that I loved the most in the world had suddenly changed up on me. It had been that way since Grant had gotten famous and turned into GT Wells.

Grant, Brooke, and I had known each other since middle school. Back then, both of them were two totally different people. At the time, Grant was in the choir at both church and school, an honor roll student, very quiet and nerdy with glasses. Brooke was more outgoing but very sweet and loving. When we first met at tryouts, she was shy and asked me to help her learn the routine. After days of working together, we clicked instantly after we both made the dance team. We became thick as thieves and were always at each other's houses.

It wasn't until freshman year that I even noticed Grant. In my mind, I saw him as off limits because I didn't want to mess up my relationship with Brooke. But when Grant asked me to the school dance, she all but begged me to go with him. That night was when I gained my first love and forgot my vow to stay away from Grant.

I fell in love with his sweet demeaner and the way he treated me like I was the most precious thing in the world to him. For the rest of high school, Grant and I were the perfect couple and made plans to have a future together. He was going to become a music teacher and chase his dreams of becoming a singer. I was going to open up a performing arts school. I had originally wanted to be a singer myself, but Grant was adamant that I was too naïve to be in the business and didn't want other men taking advantage of me. However, after graduation, those plans all changed when Grant entered a talent show and won. He went from nothing to stardom quickly, and it forever changed the man I loved and my best friend, into people I didn't recognize. Grant became GT Wells, an arrogant, rude, habitual lying-ass cheater. While Brooke became this shade throwing, interfering bitch, 'think I'm better than everybody' manager.

For the next six years, I watched the Grant and Brooke, I knew turn into the most self-centered, rude ass people I had ever seen.

"Grant, my hair is done. This is a twist out and a lot of people with natural hair wear it this way. You would know I wear my hair like this all the time if you were at home more."

"Don't start this shit, Elle! I'm not about to have you out here looking like Ms. Cellie from The Color Purple, while my name is attached to you. Look, Nya is here at the studio doing Raven's hair, and she can throw some bundles in yours after she finishes. I just text Brooke and told her to go to the hair store and get the shit Nya needs to do it. Now, take that off the rack Walmart wedding dress off and come and get something done to your head. I gotta go, but I'll see you once you get here," he ordered and hung up the phone.

Snapping my head in Brooke's direction, I said, "Really, Brooke? Why would you send him pictures of me in my wedding dress? You know, I told you I didn't want him to see me in my dress before the wedding! Then to top it off, you and your brother now want to control what I do to my own damn hair! This is too fucking much, and you know it!"

"First of all, you are a reflection of my brother, and your hair looks a hot damn mess! Secondly, that's not your wedding dress, so he hasn't seen you in it. Now come on, so we can stop at the hair store and get the shit she needs to hook your hair up. Luckily, that bush on top of your head is long enough to go without bundles once it's blown out and flat ironed. We need to get Nya to do your make-up too. My brother is right about you looking basic, Elle. People all over social media are looking at him sideways because he stays with you. At first, they let your appearance slide because you were pregnant, but now that you lost the baby, there's no excuse for you to look sloppy. Everybody thinks he needs to be with someone on his level like Raven. I'm telling you as your best friend that you need to step your game up, sis, before someone else does," Brooke stated with a smirk on her face.

Fighting back tears at her words, I headed back into the dressing room to get away from her. She knew that bringing up losing my daughter was a touchy subject for me. Even after six months, the pain of losing her hadn't let up.

I was almost six months pregnant when I lost my daughter, Ivy. Our relationship had been rocky for months before I got pregnant, due to all the rumors circulating about Grant having babies throughout the country. The only reason I had put up with his shit was because he had proposed and promised he was a changed man. We had even gone to counseling where he had revealed he was a sex addict and had started a program for his addiction. Of course, wanting to save our relationship and stand by my man, I gave him another chance.

For the first few months of my pregnancy, the old Grant was there for us. He was attentive to my needs, came straight home from the studio, and everything was perfect. What I didn't realize was he had just gotten better at hiding his dirt. The day I woke up in pain and was burning when I peed, let me know something wasn't right. Imagine my shock when the doctor told me I had an STD. I had only been with one man in my life, so I knew just who had given it to me. My blood boiled at the realization that Grant had put me and our baby at risk. That was the last straw for me. I had packed my bags and decided to leave him for good.

In my haste to get away while he was still at the studio, I tripped and fell down the stairs, causing me to lose the one person in the world I loved the most. Of course, Grant and his family along with my mother, blamed me for being reckless and killing Ivy. The whole time I was in the hospital recovering, they all yelled and cussed me out every chance they got. But no one blamed me more than I blamed myself for her death.

For months, I was in a deep depression and had grown used to the treatment I received. Hell, I felt like I deserved it for being so stupid and clumsy. I put up with Grant and everyone else's shit because it was my penance for killing my child. Everything they dished out, I deserved for not getting out of this fucked-up relationship sooner. When I was rushing around, not once did I think about my child and her safety. I was too busy being pissed off at her father and his tramps, to focus on what was going on around me. Now, my baby was gone.

"Damn, can you hurry up in there, Elle? Nya said she has another client to do this evening, so you need to come the fuck on! It's already bad GT had to pay her an extra five hundred to squeeze your ungrateful ass into her schedule!" Brooke yelled then mumbled the last sentence.

The old me would have went the fuck off on her and beat her ass, but the new me didn't even have the energy to put up a fight. So, after one last look at my dream wedding dress, I took it off. After putting on my clothes, I headed out to let my fiancé, mother, and future sister-in-law, mold me into the person they wanted me to be.

I HAD BEEN IN THE STUDIO NON-STOP FOR THE PAST THREE days, working with three clients on their albums. Two were top R&B artists named Raven & GT Wells. The other artist was Saveon, my brother, with his upcoming gospel album. Raven was alright to work with, but she had made it obvious she wanted something more from me than just lyrics and beats. I didn't believe in sleeping with artists, I was working with because the shit could get real messy. The one thing I took seriously was my craft.

GT, on the other hand, was a fucking nightmare to deal with. Half the time, he was smoking so much, he would be too high and goofy to record shit. The other half was spent in the bathroom, booth, or wherever, getting fucked and sucked by groupies. We were behind on his album because he was too busy smoking and fucking to be worried about his music.

"Damn, bruh, who put that mean look on your face," Saveon inquired as he took a swig of his water.

We had just finished his session and were catching up before I had to go and deal with GT.

"Man, trying to get my damn temper in check before I head into the studio with GT's clown ass. I'm at the point of telling his label I refuse to work with him because he's too damn flaky!"

"I've heard and seen how he works since I've been here. I'm surprised you haven't kicked him out already, to be honest with you," he responded.

Shaking my head, I said, "Naw, he's on Doom's label, and you know me and him go way back. Our friendship is the only reason I haven't whooped GT's ass and thrown him out of my studio."

"You just need to tell him what's going on before it gets out of hand. The last thing you need is for someone to record you beating the Prince of R&B's ass! You know the tabloids are already having a field day about your dating life, not to mention, all the partying you like to do. Pepper has been squashing rumors left and right about you and Raven. You got my baby working overtime on cleaning up your image. Especially, after that Kiara shit went left," Saveon added.

Shaking my head, I thought back on my situation with Kiara. She was a choreographer for a lot of artists, and we hooked up one night after a concert. Stupidly, I decided to try and entertain a situationship with her and that shit lasted all of six months. I soon realized it wasn't really me she wanted, it was my status as the hottest producer and songwriter out right now. I got tired of waking up to tags all over social media in her posts. Then everywhere we went, the paparazzi seemed to show up before we did. I knew something wasn't right about the situation, but I was trying to give her the benefit of the doubt.

The shit really hit the fan when she posted videos of me asleep and naked in her bed. Then a fucking sex tape popped up of us that I knew I didn't make. The public ate that shit up and pictures of my dick were everywhere. Not to mention, the next night, I broke up with her fame hungry ass at her birthday party. Little did I know, the hoe was recording me without my knowledge and made me look like the bad guy. Luckily, Pepper had gotten into Public Relations a few years ago instead of court reporting. She had wanted to find a way to work with Saveon, so she and the kids could travel with him on tours. After giving birth to my new niece, Joy, Pepper became my PR manager as well. Sad thing was she was earning every penny by cleaning up my messes.

"Yeah, you got that right, bruh! Every time I run into her, she creates some drama that ends up in the fucking Shade Room or Zeewiththetea! I can't even get no damn pussy in peace with her simple ass causing drama!"

"I told you sleeping with all those women was going to cause you problems. If memory serves me right, I also told you I got bad vibes from her and you needed to leave her alone. But naw, you told me I was just being paranoid and too holier than thou. But look at the position you are in now, bruh. All because she had a big booty and you loved how her mouth worked! Just because I'm saved doesn't mean I forgot the way the world works, Savior. I applaud you for trying to be with only one woman, but Kiara wasn't it, and you know it," he replied.

Before I could respond, the door opened, and Matese walked in with a mean mug on his face. Matese needed a job after he got out of jail, and I gave him a position on my security team. He dove headfirst into his position and quickly worked his way up. He was now my head of security and my personal bodyguard. Tese had also become one of my best friends, and I looked at him as a little brother.

"What's wrong with you, Tese?"

"Man, I'm telling you now, I'm about two seconds from opening up the door to Studio F and airing that bitch out! GT and his crew are getting out of hand! I had to go rescue one of their groupies because some of them can't take no for a fucking answer! She's alright and on her way home in an Uber, but something needs to be done before they fuck up your studio's reputation," Tese explained, pacing the floor.

Running a hand down my face, I tried to ease the tension and anger in my body before I beat Matese to shooting GT's whole crew. My brother gave me a look, shook his head, and commented, "Naw, bruh, I know what you are thinking, and it's not even worth it. You worked too damn hard on getting your life together. Don't let these fools take you out of character. Let me talk to them first and see if I can reason with them."

"Saveon, I'm telling you now that these are the type of assholes you can't reason with. I've been in and out of the studio all day, trying to get them to act like they have some gotdamn sense. Some people don't respond to nothing but you going upside their heads," Tese replied.

Saveon shook his head, got up with his cane, and answered,

"Yeah, but at least we can say we tried before we start beating their asses! Unlike you two, I have a wife to answer to if I get locked up. So, I at least need to show her I tried. Not to mention, I don't think my fans want to get a glimpse of the old Saveon Morrison. But for my brother, I will gladly take the hit from the public and the police."

"Naw, bruh, at least one of us needs to be kept out of this shit. You can head on home and tell Pepper to get a press release ready in case they don't listen, and I end up in jail. Right now, you are the squeaky-clean Morrison brother with a wife and family. Not to mention, you are one of the top Christian recording artist right now. Let Tese and I handle it because you have too much to lose. If it will make you feel better, I will try your kumbaya shit before I knock his teeth out. If I can try for peace, then you can do the one thing you have been putting off for months. Go over that list of female artists to sing those duets you want to do for your debut R&B album. We are supposed to start in a few months and your picky ass hasn't liked any of the artist I have sent your way," I remarked.

Saveon waved his free hand and responded, "Alright, Savior, I see you aren't going to back down. I'll look over the list and listen to the demos you gave me of female singers. Maybe I can get Pepper to help me narrow down the list. You know it took a lot of prayer and talking it over with Pepper, for me to decide adding R&B to my repertoire. I'm just glad I can now pick my own music, so I can still keep it clean and about love instead of sex. I can't wait to be your first artist on the record label. When are you going to make the big announcement about Morrison Records?"

"I'm going to do it at the afterparty, I'm throwing after the Star Awards in Vegas. Hell, everyone will be there anyway to celebrate, so it will be the perfect time. Then we can announce your move to R&B. Everyone thinks you are just working on a new Christian album and won't expect the switch. I'm happy you are finally expanding your catalog and the buzz will be great PR for my label," I replied.

Saveon nodded, smiled and said, "Yeah, and Pepper will be excited and ready to get stuff together for the party and announcement. You know she loves planning parties and spending your money. I'll let her know once I get home, so she can start on everything. But first, I'm going to walk down the hall with you and Tese because you need a buffer in case shit goes bad."

"Cool, tell sis to call me tonight, so we can go over some things. Now come on, Tese, let's see if we can get these mutherfuckers to get the hell out of here, tonight. There is no way in hell I am doing his session while he's high and his crew is acting a fucking fool!" I declared, before heading to the other side of the building where GT's studio was located.

My studio was my baby, and I was proud of every square inch of it. It wasn't your typical studio either. A lot of my artists came in from out of town, so I made sure my studio housed almost everything they needed in this building. There was a total of eight studios, two stylist offices with huge closets, a spot for hair and make-up artists, and three dance studios. I even had a small restaurant and two lounges for everyone to chill out at. Since I damn near lived here, my office had a private bathroom with a jacuzzi and large shower, and a small gym attached. I was in talks with Kevell to add on more studios and a dorm in the near future, since I was about to start adding talent to my new record label.

We were just about to pass the dance studios, when I heard something that stopped me in my tracks. A voice so pure and melodic that goosebumps formed on my arms. Saveon and I exchanged looks then both headed in the direction of the angelic voice.

"My heart aches, at every promise that you break.

No love left here since your intentions are clear.

Now our vows have been broken, with every lie you have spoken!"

THE SONG ENDED WITH HER HUMMING AS WE STEPPED INTO dance studio B. I was shocked to see GT's fiancée, Elle, humming as she did some dance moves around the floor. Even though she did choreography for GT and a lot of artists, she was almost never here. He didn't want her around the studio, so he could fuck every groupie in sight. She was sweet and had the cute average girl next door look. I always respected her because despite her being in the business, she didn't rock the bundles, fake nails, or get her ass or breasts enhanced like most.

Elle was slim with slight curves and a small pudge to her stomach with chocolate smooth skin and natural curly hair that usually was just below her shoulders. Today, however, it was straightened and fell to the middle of her back. Slanted brown eyes set off her slender face, along with a gorgeous smile that I had only seen a few times in the year I had known her. There was an innocence and genuine nature about her, and it drew you in.

Saveon and Tese both clapped and startled Elle. Matese's phone rang, and he stepped back out of the room.

"Damn, y'all scared me! I'm sorry, I was just finishing up a routine for GT's performance at the Star Awards next month. His lead dancer broke her leg, so I have to step in and take her place. If you give me five minutes, I can get my stuff and head out," she responded, taking Air Pods from her ears.

Saveon stepped forward on his cane and said, "Naw, you don't have to go. We heard you singing from the hallway. Why aren't you using your God-given talent? I mean, don't get me wrong you can definitely dance, but your voice is amazing."

"Yeah, you really got some skills, little mama. I've been around you for damn near a year and had no clue you were a singer," I added.

She blushed, shook her head, and replied, "No, I don't sing except when I'm alone. Choreography is more my lane and singing isn't something, I want to get into as a career."

"But you could though, Elle. Shit, I would love to put some words to your voice," I commented as my mind went into overdrive, creating words to put with her unique sound. Her voice reminded me of a young Mariah Carey mixed with Lauryn Hill; soulful, yet light and melodic at the same time.

Saveon nodded and added, "Yeah, Savior is right, Elle. As a matter of fact, you are exactly what I have been searching for. God must have placed me here at this time to hear you because your voice is perfect for my new album. I think our voices together would be dope as hell."

"You're joking, right? Saveon, you are one of the top artist out right now. You can have your pick of any of the talented female singers in the industry. Look, I know I can carry a tune but that's as far as I can take it. The last thing I would want to do is mess up your reputation, Savior, and your album, Saveon," she responded, half-heartedly.

I could tell there was another reason behind her refusal because I saw a flicker of hope and longing when Saveon asked her to be on his album. He was right when he said she would be perfect to partner with him on his album because I could hear their voices blending together perfectly in my head. Not to mention, possibly adding her to my company as my first female artist. Hearing her voice in my head again, I knew I had to do whatever I could to get her to sign with me. There was something special about her and her voice.

"Elle, believe me when I say that I don't fuck around when it comes to my brother's career or my music. If both of us are telling you that you have talent, then you need to listen. What's holding you back from saying yes because I can tell singing is in your blood. Is it stage fright or is someone holding you back?"

"Ain't nobody holding her back! She told you, she doesn't want to sing, so stop trying to push my girl into shit she doesn't want to do!" GT came into the room and wrapped an arm around Elle's shoulders.

I watched as she visibly tensed up at his touch. The light I saw earlier when she was singing and dancing, instantly faded away. My own hands clenched, wondering if he was laying hands on her. Looking at him, I could tell he was high as fuck and drunk off his ass. It reminded me of what Matese had told me earlier.

"I wasn't asking you, GT. What I talk about with her in my fucking building doesn't concern you. Instead of worrying about what she has going on, you need to be worried about your own shit! As a matter of fact, maybe we need to talk about what went down earlier in the studio. Since it's stopping you from recording your album."

"You can dismiss me with that shit! I'm not kissing your ass like these other mutherfuckers in this industry! I got awards, bitches, and money just like you do! The only reason I'm in your shit is because Doom has me locked into a bullshit ass contract! I'm a mutherfucking boss and can produce and write my own shit!" he ranted, slurring his words.

I stepped toward him, but Saveon grabbed my arm while Elle turned to him and ordered, "Grant, stop! You are drunk and don't know or mean what you are saying! Savior, I'm sure once he sobers up, everything can be straightened out. Let me take him home before things get out of hand."

"Yeah, bruh, you don't need to get into shit before the Star Awards next month. You are up for five awards, and the last thing you need is bad press. Let him sleep that shit off and you calm down. Tomorrow, you can put his punk ass in his place," Saveon whispered to me.

Gritting my teeth, I looked at his drunk ass and realized he wasn't even present, and it wouldn't be a fair fight. He was wobbling and his eyes were tight as shit.

"Take his ass home but tell him he can't come back here

until I talk to Doom. Elle, make sure you think about the offer from me and Saveon. Your voice is amazing, and you could do big things with it. Don't let anybody tell you differently because they are being selfish. No one should ruin your shot at living your dreams or stopping you from being happy, little mama."

Elle didn't say anything in response but gave me a small head nod and smile. GT was mumbling as she guided him away from me toward the door. When I looked up, I realized Brooke and Raven were standing there watching the whole thing. Both of them were sneering at Elle, and I could see the jealousy written all over their faces.

"Savior, I hope you know I'm calling Doom as soon as I get home! My brother is one of the top artist in R&B right now and is making you a lot of money. GT is a star and should be treated like one. He is going to hear about how you treated my brother, today!" Brooke threatened.

Brooke and Doom were an item, so I knew she was going to be running her mouth about what I said, but I didn't give a fuck. Doom was a friend, but I ran my business the way I saw fit. "Is that supposed to scare me, sweetheart? Cause believe me, being Doom's in-house pussy won't make him choose your side over his money. Just a fact, I thought you should know before you made that call. Now, get your brother and his entourage the fuck out of my building before I start shooting and asking questions later!"

Brooke huffed and stomped out, leaving Elle to take the brunt of carrying an increasingly unstable Grant. I nodded toward Matese, who had just come in and was taking in the scene. Following my eyes, he nodded and took over helping her get GT out of the room. Elle looked back and mouthed "thank you" before she headed out of the dance studio.

Raven came sashaying over to Saveon and me. She then latched on to Saveon, pressing her breasts against his arm. Raven batted her eyes at him, pouted, then whined, "Saveon, I thought I was in the running for doing a duet on your new album? You know, I have been looking into other genres. Elle is a choreographer and knows nothing about singing. Plus, why would you pick her when I am one of the top female artist out right now! I have over fifty million followers, and I'm in talks for my own reality show. Everybody loves me because I am a single mom, beautiful, and make my own money. We could make millions together just off our names alone, Saveon. There is no way your album will be a success with a no-name like Elle. How about I call my manager, and we can have her hook up a deal to put money in both our pockets. Then, I will do everything and anything in my power to make our partnership pleasant for both of us."

Saveon frowned, pushed her off him and said, "Excuse me, but you know I'm a happily married man, and you're trying to push your titties all up on me, thinking it's going to sway me into working with you. I was trying to save your feelings, but you want to down somebody else who has real talent. That lets me know you're insecure and on some jealous shit! Let me school you real quick because there are a lot of reasons, I would never work with you, Raven. One, your voice is mediocre at best, and I need someone who can blow. See, the reason you are so popular isn't because you have talent, it's because you perform in your bra and panties, hunching on half your audience, and shaking your funky ass. Which brings me to reason number two of my point. I'm a Christian singer, and you are known as the Jezebel of R&B, who sleeps with all of the people she works with, despite them being married or not. My wife is a gift from God, and I love and respect her too much to have you trying to break up our happy home because you want to be messy. I take my vows seriously, Satan, so it's a no for me."

"You don't have to be rude, damn! Nobody was trying to fuck you, Saveon! I mean, you cute and all, but I have my sights set on someone else a little closer to you. I'm just being a woman about mine and trying to secure my bag," she retorted, with a scowl on her face.

Scoffing, my brother headed toward the door and said, "Let me get out of here before I snatch your disrespectful ass up! Got me in here cussing and having evil thoughts about choking hoes and shit because I'm in the same room with you! My name ain't Jesus, and I damn sure not trying to be Captain Save-a-Hoe! Yeah, bruh, you got this shit! I'm heading home to pray that he takes all hoes and snakes out of my path and yours! You see I'm still a work in progress, and God knows my heart and trigger finger. Call me later, Savior!"

"Alright, bruh, tell Matese to head back this way once he makes sure GT is off my property," I responded, trying hard not to laugh.

Saveon kept walking and threw up his hand to acknowledge what I said. I turned to Raven, who was staring at my dick print and licking her lips.

"You can stop that shit because you know I would never take it there with you. Now in case you didn't understand what my brother was saying, there is no chance in hell he will put you on his album. If you want to continue working with me on your own music, I suggest you change your attitude or you will end up like GT, which is out on his ass without a producer. So, put your high mileage pussy away and stop throwing it at every man that comes in here. Especially me and my happily married brother."

"I don't throw it at every man, Savior, just the ones who I want the most. You act like its wrong for me to go after what and who I want. I'm single and it's my pussy, so I can fuck whoever I want to. Who I really want to fuck is you, Savior, but you keep playing games by telling me you don't sleep with women you work with. My album is almost finished, and then there won't be any excuse you can use for us not to be together," she retorted.

Shaking my head, I headed to the door because this hoe was delusional. She eye-fucked me as I walked to the door. Raven thought she had the upper hand because I was walking away, but she had shit all fucked-up.

Turning around, I ordered, "Since you can't take a fucking hint, I guess I will have to show you better than I can tell you. Take the rest of the week to get it through your head, that I wouldn't fuck you if you were the last piece of pussy in the world. A mutherfucker would rather die from blue balls than stick my dick in your Venus Flytrap pussy! Now, get the fuck out of here before I have Matese throw your trifling ass out!"

Before she could reply, I headed out the door and down the

hall. I had to rework the studio schedule and call Doom and let him know what the fuck his artists were up to. I'm sure he had already gotten an earful from Brooke, but he needed to hear my side and get his people in line before I did that shit for him.

As I passed one of the glass windows, I saw Elle and Matese pushing GT into the car. My eyes unintentionally roved over the curve of Elle's ass, as she bent over to buckle him in. I couldn't help but to adjust myself as thoughts of bending her over in the booth while she hit those high notes I heard earlier. Not liking where my thoughts were headed, I shook the thoughts from my head.

Once she was in the car and my view of her was gone, I headed toward my office to take care of business. Elle's voice kept singing in my head and creating words to go with her sweet sound. I made up my mind that I would convince her to work with my brother and me. Her voice and Saveon's together would make us all a lot of money. No matter what I had to do, the duet between Elle and Saveon was happening.

I had already booked Saveon and I some studio time in Vegas. We were going to start working on his album during the weeks leading up to the Star Awards. I would have loved to see about adding the duet between he and Elle, to his performance there. It would have given people a sneak peek to what my brother could bring to R&B and introduce the world to Elle. With the official announcement for my label, Saveon venturing into R&B could be at the after party, and God willing, signing Elle as my first female artist. In my mind; I could already picture them on stage together making magic. If I wanted my vision to become a reality, I had to find a way to get Elle to work with me. That would only leave me a few short weeks to convince her that she had something special before the awards show. The only thing standing in my way was her punk ass fiancé, GT.

MATESE

I WAS TIRED AS HELL COMING BACK FROM THE STUDIO. THE first thing I smelled when I hit the door, was Catrina's cooking. I smiled because I couldn't wait to eat and spend some time with her. In the past few months, we had moved in and taken our relationship to the next level. She treated me like a king and made me think about having a future with her.

When I walked into the kitchen, Catrina had the music going and was dancing in her pink scrubs as she cooked. She was twerking her small ass off, but that was my baby.

Catrina was slim, bordering more toward the skinny side. She was light skin with light brown eyes, thin pink lips, and brownish-blond medium-length hair. Trina only had a handful of breast and ass, but it all looked good on her. Not to mention, not only was she beautiful on the outside but on the inside as well.

Walking up behind Catrina, I wrapped my arms around her

and started kissing on her neck. "Damn, baby you got it smelling good as fuck in here! What you cooking?"

"Lemon pepper baked chicken, sautéed spinach, and brown rice. I even stopped and picked up that key lime pie you like from Sandy's Bakery. Why don't you go and hop in the shower while I get everything on plates? My shift starts in a few hours, and I want to talk to you about something before I head into work," she replied, pushing away from me to look in the oven.

Frowning, I responded, "Naw, what's wrong, Trina? Your voice doesn't sound right."

"Just take your shower, baby, and we can talk about it over dinner," she answered, before turning around to get the plates together.

Shaking my head, I went took a shower, and came back down. The table was set, and we sat down and started eating in silence. As I ate and drank my beer, I watched Trina and could tell something was on her mind. She was pushing around the food on her plate and chewing on her bottom lip. Putting my fork down, I asked, "Alright, Trina, what's going on? You have stalled long enough, and I need to know what's wrong."

"I think, I might be pregnant, Tese. For the past few days, I have been throwing up and sick to my stomach. I want you to know that this wasn't planned, and I've always taken my birth control on time for years. I'm not one-hundred percent sure if I'm pregnant or not, but it's a strong possibility. Tonight, I'll get a test done at work to give you a definite answer," she rambled.

Staring at Trina in shock, I was trying to process what she was saying. Since we had moved in together, we had stopped using condoms because she was on birth control. Hell, she wasn't lying about taking them because Trina faithfully popped them every morning. I knew we were taking a chance every time I made love to her, but I thought the odds of her getting pregnant would be low.

"Have you had any of the other symptoms yet?"

"My breasts are sore, and I've had to pee a lot lately. I wasn't even the one who picked up on the symptoms. Mashelle pointed them out to me when I threw up at lunch, today. Fucked up since I'm the one who's a nurse, right? But I've been so busy with work, school, and clinicals, I just didn't have time to notice what was going on with my own body. Tese, I know we haven't talked about kids and this wasn't planned, but I don't know if I can have an abortion," Trina stated, with tears in her eyes.

Standing up, I walked over to her and pulled her into my arms. Placing a kiss on her lips, I responded, "Trina, if you are pregnant, there's no way in hell I would want you to kill our child. Am I shocked, hell yes, but I knew the chances of you getting pregnant, when I started making love to you without wrapping up. Hell, we live together, and I love you. Why wouldn't I want our baby. We are both grown and make more than enough money to bring a child into this world. You are almost finished with school and about to become a Nurse Practitioner. Alexis already has a position lined up for you at the clinic, that has daycare for their employees. I know she will adjust your schedule to accommodate the pregnancy, so you won't have to worry about losing your job. I'm making damn good money with Savior, and he is planning on being in town more, so I can be here with you through the pregnancy. So, stop crying because you know I can't stand that shit, and go find out if you're having my baby or not. Naw, fuck that, I'm going with you. I can wait in the lobby until you get the results. You aren't alone in this, Catrina; I will be here every step of the way."

She smiled, then stood on her toes and kissed me. Pulling her closer to me, I deepened the kiss and felt my dick grow as desire took over. Her watch started beeping, bringing us out of our make out session.

"Damn, I wish I could call out tonight, but I only have a few more hours left, and if I want to meet you in Vegas, those have to be completed first. I can't wait for some vacation time with my man. One month off sounds really good right now," Trina remarked as she pulled away from the kiss.

Pecking her lips one more time, I said, "Yeah, you deserve it, baby. You've worked your ass off for that degree, and I'm glad you are taking some time off before you start working in your new position. Plus, I can't wait to get you alone for a whole month in Vegas. I made sure we have enough security to take care of everyone, so I can spend as much time with you as possible. Now, let's head out of here to see if you will be able to kick it with us there or have to sit your ass down in the room somewhere!"

"Excuse you! Even if I am pregnant, I bet I will be twerking right along with Pepper and Mashelle! You got me messed up!" she barked.

I laughed as we both got ready and headed out of the house. The whole way to the hospital, we talked about our upcoming trip to Vegas and her graduation afterward. As she went on and on about the test, she needed to take and stuff she wanted to get for the trip, I watched her and felt a feeling I couldn't explain, burning in my chest.

Catrina had a glow about her and radiated so much passion and love, that it made me feel like I was drowning at times. I had only felt this feeling once before and that was with my ex, Janiyah. Trina and Janiyah were as different as night and day, so to compare them was moot. These normal, everyday moments of being with Trina, made me realize I wanted something more with her. I wanted her to be my wife and not just because she might be carrying my child either. It was just as simple as I never wanted to be without her.

"Do you ever think about getting married?"

"Where did that come from, Matese? If this is because of me possibly being pregnant, then the answer is no. This isn't the fifties, and I would never want a man to marry me because I was pregnant. Our relationship works just fine as it is, and I want you to be one-hundred percent sure when you do ask me to be your wife. Plus, you aren't ready yet, Tese. You have some unre-solved issues with your past to deal with. When you give me your last name, I don't want another woman in our marriage. Especially, one you still have feelings for, but won't admit it," she answered.

Breathing out deeply, I knew exactly what and who she meant, but the shit still pissed me off. Catrina always was pressing me to deal with the anger and resentment I felt toward Janiyah, but to me, it wasn't that simple. I didn't want to deal with or talk about anything that had to do with my ex-girlfriend. She wasn't worth my time or energy anymore! Janiyah had betrayed me in ways no woman, who claimed to love a man should. When I got locked up on a bogus drug charge, I was only supposed to serve a year in jail. My sister, Mashelle's ex-fiancé, Theo, made sure to keep piling on more charges to control her, every time I was about to get released.

One year turned into five; stuck in limbo at Theo's whim. Every day I thought he would make up something that would send me to prison for good, and at any moment I would be moved to prison on some heavier shit to serve double digits. It was the threat he held over my sister and my head, every time Mashelle did something he didn't like. Janiyah knew the shit I was going through and that it wasn't my fault. However, it didn't seem to make a difference to her because she still left me high and dry.

Janiyah lied about hanging in there with me while I did my time. Instead, she started fucking my ex-best friend, Yo. Imagine my shock when I went to her house after I got out to start a new life with her, and she opens the door with a newborn baby in her arms. One who looked just like my best friend. Not to mention, he came out in a towel with a smirk on his face and told me to stay away from his family, before slamming the door in my face. After that, Janiyah and Yo were dead to me, erased from my mind and heart.

"Trina, I told you before that Janiyah doesn't mean shit to me, which when means she is not in our relationship! I didn't bring up marriage because you might be pregnant. I brought it up because I love you and want to spend the rest of my life with you. I'm not asking you to marry me right now, I was just trying to see what your thoughts were on the topic."

"I hear what you are saying, Tese, but I still think you are in denial about your feelings. I will let it go for now because we have other issues we need to deal with. But for the record, I would love to be your wife, when you are ready to ask me," she replied.

I smiled as we pulled into the garage at the hospital, parked, and headed inside. Trina went upstairs to get tested, and I waited in the lobby downstairs. Just to pass the time, I grabbed a magazine with no intentions of really reading it. My thoughts were on Trina being pregnant with my baby.

It wasn't a secret that my sister, Mashelle, and I had fucked-up childhoods. We always dreamed of having big families of our own and getting to do things with them that we missed out on growing up. Just thinking about a mini version of me or Trina, had me contemplating going ring shopping tomorrow. She was right about one thing; it was time for me to get over my issues and fully commit to her. Vegas would be the perfect place to propose to Catrina and start our future together.

Putting the magazine down, I pulled out my phone and texted Savior and Mashelle. I asked them if they would go with me to help pick out a ring for Trina. After they both responded yes, I pulled up some rings on my phone and started browsing to see what caught my eye. I was sitting for about twenty minutes going crazy, trying to figure out what kind of ring Trina would like, when I felt something tugging on my leg.

"Mr., can I have a dollar, so I can get some chips? I'm hungry," a little boy asked.

Looking down at him, he looked as if he was about three years old; light skin with dark brown eyes, clean but on the skinny side. He looked familiar but I couldn't put my finger on who he reminded me of. I looked around and didn't see any adults with him. It made me wonder if he was lost.

"Yeah, I'll give you a dollar, but where is your mama and daddy and how old are you? You know you shouldn't be here by yourself, little man."

"I'm almost five, and I don't have a daddy! My mama is in the bathroom with my baby sister! Now, are you gonna give me the dollar or what?" he demanded.

Reaching into my pocket, I peeled off a few ones and handed it to him and said, "I shouldn't give you nothing since you don't know how to ask people politely. Now, I'm going to give you a chance to at least say thank you, after you get your chips and something to drink. Do you want to get some for your sister too?"

"Landa is a baby, she drinks milk! She can't have soda, but I can share my chips with her cause she's too little to eat a whole bag. Thank you for the money though!" he responded as he took the ones from my hand and got what he wanted from the machine.

He came back and handed me the bottle of soda to open, sat down beside me, and started eating his chips. I kept looking around to see when his mama was going to come and get him, but so far, no one looked as if they were.

"What's your name? Do they feed you at home?"

"Maurice, but my mama calls me Rece. I like that better because I just do. My mama's boyfriend calls me little bastard, but I don't answer to that. He doesn't like me because he said I'm yellow and a punk like my daddy. He says my daddy didn't want me, so he left. We eat but not as much as I want to because mama's boyfriend said he ain't feeding another man's seed. So, mama has to wait for her stamps to come, and she buys me snacks I can hide in my room and eat when he's tripping. We've been at the hospital all day because mama got sick. We haven't eaten yet cause she ain't got no money, just a bus pass," he mumbled in between stuffing his face with chips.

My jaw clenched along with my fist at the little boy's words. Whoever this boyfriend was, was fucked up for calling this little boy out of his name! His mama was trifling for allowing him to get away with it!

"Well, don't listen to him because you are not a little bastard, he is! Also, don't say that word again, because only dumb ass people use it. Any man that disrespects a child is the one who is a punk! Look, here's my card, if you ever feel like he might hurt you or your mama, give me a call. Damn, you ate those chips fast as hell! Let me grab you one more bag."

He nodded as he downed the soda and started watching the cartoons that were on the television on the side of the room with the kids' stuff. I walked back over to the machine and decided to get him a few bags of chips and cookies, so he could take them home with him.

"Rece, where have you been! I told you to wait for me right outside the bathroom door! I was all over this hospital looking for you!" screamed a familiar voice.

My whole body froze as I realized who the voice belonged to. Whipping around, I saw the woman I thought I would spend the rest of my life with, yelling at Maurice, with my best friend's daughter in her arms. Now, I realized who the little boy looked like. He was the spitting image of Janiyah. The only thing he didn't have was her smooth chocolate skin complexion.

My eyes couldn't help but to move over her body as she continued to chastise Maurice. She was slimmer than I remembered, but still had a nice shape that used to be molded to me at night. Janiyah had cat like dark brown eyes and full lips. Her face was thinner and paler than the last time I saw her. There were bags under her eyes, and I could tell something was going on with her because she looked tired.

"Hello, Janiyah," I stated, walking up to her and Maurice.

Her whole body stiffened as her head snapped around, and she stared at me with fear in her eyes. I frowned up because I didn't like the reaction, she had toward me. I had never done anything to her, so she shouldn't fear me. But then again, guilt was a mutherfucker when you know you did somebody wrong. Janiyah did me dirty as fuck, so I hoped the guilt was eating her alive.

"Matese, what are you doing here?" she answered shakily before moving her daughter to her other hip.

I replied, "Your son asked me for some money to get something from the machine because he was hungry. I didn't see anyone with him, so I thought I would stay with Maurice until someone came to get him. My girlfriend works here, and I'm waiting on her to come downstairs."

Maurice looked between the both of us as we stared at each other. The feelings I had buried deep within me for her, threatened to bubble up to the top as I stared at the woman who used to be my everything. I couldn't help but to think about the fact that the baby she was holding should have been mine, as well as her son. Her daughter was all Yo and looked as if she was a little over a year old. But her son was her twin, and at almost five, he was very smart and mature for his age. It made me wonder who his father was since he said he wasn't Yo's. Frowning, I started thinking about the timeline.

Suddenly, my eyes snapped to Maurice and then back to Janiyah. The truth was in her eyes along with tears. My blood boiled as I thought about the implications of just how deep Janiyah's betrayal ran. Before I could go the fuck off on her, she held her hand up and shook her head.

"Maurice, go throw that bag in the trash over there by the door," she ordered.

Maurice got up and answered, "Yes, ma'am."

"Matese, please, not here. I know I have a lot to explain, but we need to talk in private before I tell him. Please, he needs to hear it from me, first," she whispered.

Stepping closer to her, I growled low enough so Maurice couldn't hear, "Bitch, you just can't help fucking me over every chance you get! Please, tell me you haven't been hiding my son from me for almost five years! You can't be that damn scandalous, Niyah!"

"Matese, baby, come here!" I heard Catrina yell from behind me.

I turned away from Janiyah and saw Trina coming toward me, smiling brighter than I had ever seen before. She had a piece of paper in her hands, and I knew it was her results. Turning back around, I looked back at Janiyah to see her reaction, but she and the kids were gone. My fist clenched when I realize she had run the first chance she got.

Trina grabbed my arm and said, "Baby, what's wrong? You look upset."

The last thing I wanted to do was show her how upset I was, especially if she was pregnant. I needed to talk to Janiyah and find out the truth about Maurice's paternity, before I brought it up to Catrina. Kissing her on the forward to help calm myself down, I responded, "Naw, baby, I just thought I saw somebody I knew. Did you find out the results yet?"

"Um, yes, they are in this envelope. I didn't want to look at them without you," she answered as she handed it to me, and I opened it.

Reading the results, I smiled. Looking at Trina, I felt closer to her than ever before. I grabbed her, pulled her into my body, not caring that we were in a public lobby. I kissed her with every bit of love I had in me. By the time we pulled away, we were both breathing heavy.

"You are having my baby, Trina, and I have never loved you more than I do at this moment."

"I love you too, Tese! I'm so glad you are happy about the baby! My shift is about to start, I have to head back up. I'm just excited we are about to be first-time parents together. Tracy is going to cover the second half of my shift, so I can come home early, and we can celebrate. You head home and save me some dessert. Love you, baby!" she beamed before giving me a kiss.

After saying our goodbyes, I watched her head up the stairs until she disappeared from my sight. I didn't want to break her heart by telling her, she most likely wasn't the first woman to give me a child. I had to find Janiyah fast and find out if Maurice was my son or not.

One Month Later

"Damn, Niyah, I told you to pick up the deposits at the clubs and drop them off to Henry! How the hell could you screw something so simple up! Now, I have to fix your fuck up before I go! I swear, the only thing you are good for is spreading your fucking legs and having babies!" Yo screamed at me as he got dressed to go to one of the strip clubs he owned.

Yo owned three strip clubs and two regular clubs all over Nashville. After Matese got locked up, Yo took his place in the streets, making enough money to fund his dreams of being a club owner. Once that happened, he gave up the drug game and had some of the best clubs in the city. I ran errands for him, so he could spend time fucking half the groupies and strippers in the state.

Sitting on the bed feeding Yolanda, I tried to stay silent so that he could say his piece and leave. After years of being forced to be with Yo, I was finally done. It took me five years to find the thing he had been holding over my head, and I knew where it was. Now, Yo couldn't use it to keep me away from Matese. It was time for him to know the truth and make him understand why I betrayed him. The first thing was getting Yo out of here, so I could take my kids and leave this nightmare behind. The failed pickups at his clubs wasn't a mistake. I needed Yo all the way on the other side of town while we got away.

"I'm sorry, baby, but Landa was running a fever, so I ran to the store to get her meds and brought her straight back here to make sure she was okay."

"Well, alright, but don't let that shit happen again, Niyah! As my woman, it's your job to make sure my money is picked up and deposited on time. Make sure you fix me some wings and put them in the microwave, so I can eat them when I get home from the club in the morning. You know after fucking, I get hungry. Since you on your period and shit, I need to get one of them hoes down at the strip club to get me right. You just make sure my daughter gets better. My mama is picking her up tomorrow to get pictures done. I'll be back in the morning before she gets here," he stated as he kissed Landa on the cheek, then headed out of the house.

I sat there for a few minutes, making sure he was gone and gathering up my courage to take the steps to finally leave him. Yo had taken away so much from me, and I was tired of losing everything because of him. I lost Matese because of Yo's treachery, and my son lost out on knowing his father. My health was fucked-up, as well as my appearance because of the shit he had put me through over the years.

He loved to verbally abuse me about the stretch marks and

cellulite I had accumulated after having Maurice and Yolanda. The worse thing about the mess I was in, is that it was hurting my child. Because Maurice belonged to Tese, Yo was mean to him. He never hit him, but the verbal abuse and being cruel to him were his go-to methods of torture. I saw the toll it was taking on my son's self-esteem. No matter what, I had to get Maurice the hell away from here before he was damaged beyond help.

Shaking my head, I stood up and placed a sleeping Landa on the bed while I grabbed the bag I had hidden in the closet. Unzipping it, I pulled out the card I had gotten from Maurice once I ran from the hospital a month ago.

That day was the day I decided it was time to get my life together for not only myself but for my kids. I was tired of just existing and being unhappy. Over the years, the secrets and lies had taken a toll on me both mentally and physically. Not to mention, I was tired of my son being treated badly by a man, who wasn't even his father. Maurice deserved to know that he had a father, who was a good man and would love him unconditionally. If it was the last thing I did, I was going to make sure my son had the father he deserved. Matese needed his son and to learn the truth about what really went down all those years ago.

Pulling out my phone, I looked up Savior Morrison's website. I knew wherever he was, Matese would be there also since he was Savior's bodyguard. When I saw they were in Vegas for the Star Awards, I went to my phone and booked the first available flight they had. It was in first class, but I didn't care about the price because I had been stealing money from Yo over the past month to fund our escape. I also booked a suite at the hotel that the gossip blogs said most of the stars were staying at for the awards show. The bag had cash, a prepaid card with the bulk of the money I had stolen, and a few things to tide us over until we settled into the hotel. I made sure the bag looked half-empty, so Yo didn't get suspicious in case he ran across the bag.

"Mama, where are we going?" Maurice asked as he walked in, drinking a juice box.

He only was able to eat extra food and stuff when Yo was away from the house. I had a hidden mini fridge and box full of snacks and juices in his room, so my son wouldn't go without. Without Yo's knowledge, I had applied for food stamps and used them to make sure Maurice didn't go hungry. Yo only cared about and paid for food for Yolanda and himself. I ate while I was cooking and when he was away. The only time he even paid for me to eat was when I was pregnant with our daughter.

"We are going on a short trip, Rece. Go to your room and pick out two toys you can take with you. Then come back in here, so we can leave, okay."

"Yes, ma'am," he stated, then ran back toward his room.

I got Landa dressed as she slept, then dressed myself, and called an Uber to pick us up. Yo never allowed me to use his cars, and I wouldn't anyway because he had trackers on them. The last thing I needed was for Yo to find out where I was going before I could get to Matese and tell him what was going on.

"Where the fuck you think you are going, Niyah? Do you think I am stupid or something? That I wouldn't notice that money was missing from my safe and that you have been acting funny the past few weeks? Bitch, you got to be fucking crazy to think that I would let you leave me and take my damn daughter with you! I told you years ago, that there would be no leaving once I stuck my dick in your stupid ass! Now, put that shit back, before you make me do something, we both regret!" Yo ordered as he walked into the room.

Cussing myself out in my head, a sense of dread and fear came over me as I looked at Yo. He had never beaten me, but he had shit hanging over my head to keep me in line. But now that I knew where the dirt was buried, it was time for me to break free. Whatever I had to do to get myself and babies out of this mess. It was a good thing I had a contingency plan in case Yo caught me. I just hoped he believed it.

"Yo, I was just getting Landa's bag ready for tomorrow. You said your mama was coming to get her, so I wanted to make sure I had everything packed. Since I knew you would be out all night, I figured I would take Maurice to stay with my mama, so he wouldn't disturb you. As for the money, I used it to pay for your surprise party. If you look in my second drawer, you will see the contracts for the club and all the vendors who are working at your party. Hell, call your mama, and she will tell you I've been planning it for the past two months. You just had to ruin it by being paranoid!"

"Alright, let me call my mama cause we both know how much of a lying and conniving bitch you are! I haven't whooped your ass before, but I promise if you are on some sneaky shit, I'm killing you, hoe!" he threatened as he phoned his mama.

He started talking to her as he paced the floor in the bathroom. I wasn't lying about the surprise party, so it was a believable excuse. I knew his mama was about to tell him the same thing I just did, but I wasn't taking any chances. Easing myself closer to the bed, I picked up Landa, so I could get the hell out of here. This was my chance to get away, and I was going to take it. Yo was crazy, and I knew he would kill me without blinking an eye. He had guns hidden throughout the house, and I had no clue where they were. His mama was long-winded, so I knew he would be occupied for a minute. I was mad as hell; we lived out in the middle of nowhere and it was going to take the Uber a minute to get here. I was whispering all kinds of prayers it would get here soon.

Once I eased out of the room, I headed toward Maurice's room to grab him and climb out of his bedroom window. It was close to the street, so we could hop in the Uber and get the hell away from here. Before I got to his bedroom door, I was grabbed around the neck and yanked back into the master bedroom. I almost dropped Landa as Yo pushed me to the ground, but she was quickly yanked from me and placed on the bed. It was a good thing she was a heavy sleeper because I didn't want her to watch me be killed by her father.

Yo pressed the gun to my head and scowled down at me and growled, "You really are a stupid bitch! I knew as soon as I turned my back, you would run and tell on yourself! Don't think I don't know about your little meetup with Matese either! Our deal was that you were supposed to stay away from him, or I would destroy his life for good! I guess seeing him made you forget that part, huh?"

"Please, Yo, I'm sorry! I just wanted to take Maurice to his father, and I was going to come back! You said you don't want him here, so I thought I would leave him with Matese and you would be happier!" I countered, hoping it would help my case.

Yo laughed and pressed the gun harder to my temple and responded, "I don't believe you, Niyah! I told you that everything that is yours belongs to me! That includes that little bastard back in the room! Since you can't understand that shit, I guess it's time for me to kill him, so he won't be a problem. But first, I'm going to beat your ass like I should have before!"

"No!" I screamed as he hit me across the face with the gun.

I felt blood running down my cheek, as pain exploded in my temple. Covering my head, I prayed he wouldn't kill me and tried to think of a way to kill him before he could get to Maurice as blows rained down on my back and arms.

Pow!

Flinching, I waited for the pain to take over my body as a gunshot went off. But when I didn't feel anything, I knew something else had happened. I heard sniffling and looked in the direction of the door. Maurice was standing there with a gun at his feet, shaking with a look of pure terror on his face as he stared at a bloody Yo on the floor.

I crawled to him and grabbed the gun in case Yo woke up. My phone pinged, and I reached into my pocket and saw that the Uber was about to be here in fifteen minutes.

Pulling Rece into my arms, I whispered, "It's okay, baby. You were just protecting your mama. Don't look at him! Go into your room and get the toys I told you to grab. We are leaving here and never coming back."

"Yes, ma'am. Sorry, I peed on myself," he said robotically, in a daze.

Looking down, I saw the urine on the floor and the telltale spot on his shorts. I knew he was more than likely in shock, and it crushed my soul. My bullshit had damaged my baby in so many ways. I felt someone tugging on me, and I jumped, pointing the gun in that direction. When I looked, it was a sleepy Landa with bloody feet from walking in the puddle forming around her father's body. I needed to get them out of here, fast.

"Rece, take your sister in the bathroom and both of you step in the tub and rinse off. Stay in there, and I will bring you some clothes. Go, now!"

"Yes, ma'am," he replied as he grabbed Landa's hand and pulled her with him.

I crept over to Yo to see if he was still breathing. His chest wasn't moving, and blood was pouring from a hole in his chest. Running, I grabbed the bag I had packed earlier, a onesie for Landa, then a pair of pants and shirt for Rece, and a dress for myself. After getting all of us cleaned off, dressed, and bandaging my face up, we ran outside just as the Uber pulled up. I put the kids inside, then ran and tossed the gun into the small pond behind the house. As I passed Yo's car, I saw the deposit bag stuffed full. Grabbing it, I stuffed it in my purse and climbed in the Uber. Making a small detour to the check cashing center, I put as much of the cash onto the prepaid card I had already filled up over the weeks with money stolen from Yo.

Once we got dropped off at the airport, we had moments to spare before the flight took off. Luckily, I didn't have any baggage to check, so we were quickly escorted to our first-class seats. My babies and I were silent until the plane was safely off the ground and in the air. Landa went to sleep, but Rece had a death grip on my arm as he stared out the window.

"Baby, I'm so sorry you had to do that. I promise you; I will never let someone treat you like that ever again," I whispered in his ear.

He turned to me with a look I never wanted to see on his young face ever again and responded, "He was hurting you! I didn't want you to die. Will I get in trouble for killing him?"

"No, baby, he's not dead. You just hurt him. Rece, look, you can't tell anybody about what happened tonight. If somebody asks you what happened, tell them you didn't see anything because you were in your room with the headphones on, okay? Promise me, baby."

Frowning, he replied, "But you told me never to lie, mommy. Wouldn't that be lying?"

"Yes, but sometimes, we have to tell lies to protect the people that we love. So, please do this for me, okay, Rece?" I reiterated.

Finally, he nodded his head and said, "Okay, mommy, I promise. Where are we going?"

"We are going to see your father, Rece, he is going to help keep us safe. Remember, I told you he was the man you met at the hospital. Well, he is in a city called Las Vegas, and we are flying there now," I explained.

Maurice looked thoughtfully then asked, "Do you think he will help us? He seemed really mad at you when we were at the hospital."

"He wasn't mad, baby. Your father was just surprised. Why don't you put your headphones on and watch one of the movies until they serve us something to eat? Before you know it, we will be in Vegas, and you can get to know your father. I promise, he will keep us safe, so don't worry about anything, Rece," I reassured him.

Rece smiled slightly, but I could tell he was still messed up from what happened earlier. Once he was engrossed in his movie, I leaned back into my seat and thought about what had just happened less than two hours ago. Yo was either dead or close to dead when I left. As soon as someone found his body, they would be looking for me and my babies. His mama was a force to be reckoned with, and I'm sure she wouldn't waste any time pointing the authorities my way. Not to mention, if Yo survived, he would be out for blood and wouldn't hesitate to kill me or my son without blinking an eye.

Matese was my only hope, and I just prayed that he would hear me out and forgive me for the secrets I kept and for betraying him when he was locked up. He had no clue that what I did was for his protection and to save his life.

I just hoped Matese didn't turn us away before he heard me out. Our lives depended on him in more ways than one.

"You need to control your bitch, GT, before I control her for you!" Raven ranted as she patted our son's back and handed him over to the nanny.

The last thing I needed was to have Raven pissed off at me. So far, she had been the perfect side chick. She never caused me any drama, and we both fucked who we wanted to without getting jealous. Neither one of us wanted to be together permanently, but we loved to fuck each other and experiment sexually. Something Elle's boring ass wouldn't be down for, no matter how much she loved me. The only problem that came from Raven's and my situationship was the fact that both of her sons were mine.

Don't get me wrong, I loved my boys, but if Elle ever found out I had a three-year-old and a five-month-old baby, she would leave me for good. Which is why I lied to Elle and told her my flight was delayed, and I wouldn't be in Vegas until tomorrow.

But in fact, I was already here in Vegas with Raven and my kids. Elle arrived yesterday, and Brooke had made her a reservation at the Mirage, which is where she was waiting for me. Raven was staying at Caesars Palace, so I could spend time with my sons and not chance running into Elle. This sneaking around shit was starting to take a toll on me.

Elle was my everything, but I was a superstar and expected to have a certain lifestyle. Monogamy and sex symbol didn't go together in this industry, but she didn't seem to get that. I didn't even want to get married, but it was the only way to make sure I had a hold on her, especially after she lost our daughter, Ivy.

Every chance I got, I reminded her of the fact that she was the cause of my daughter dying. Even though I knew my actions contributed to her death, using the guilt to hold onto Elle had made controlling her easier. We didn't argue like we had before, and I was able to get away with more than I ever had in our relationship. Now, I just had to calm Raven down, so she wouldn't give out information that would destroy my relationship.

"Raven, I told you that Elle isn't interested in working with Savior and Saveon. I told her a long time ago that singing couldn't be her career if she plans to be with me. So, you are getting stressed out for nothing, baby."

"That's easy for you to say because you think you have little Ms. Elle in control! But we are talking about Savior Morrison, one of the top producers and songwriters in the industry. Not to mention, his brother, who is the top Christian artist out right now. They seem bound and determined to get her on Saveon's record, GT. These men are both powerful and get what they want, and they want her! Look at you, Doom sided with them about kicking you out of the studio! Now, your new album has been shelved until Doom decides to hook you up with another producer. So, don't tell me you have control of the situation when we both know, you don't!" she ranted.

My jaw clenched at the reminder of my hard work going down the drain because of Savior's jealousy and arrogance. I knew he was pressed because I was getting pussy thrown at me more than he was, and because my name was on everybody's lips. My title as the Prince of R&B was solidified and he just needed to get with the fucking program!

"Don't bring that shit up again, Raven! I was the one who didn't want to work with Savior anymore! I don't have time for him to order me around just because it's his fucking studio. But don't worry, I already have a few producers lined up, who want to work with me after I get back home. For now, I'm up for four awards, performing live, and there are a ton of parties in the next few weeks, leading up to the Star Awards. Are the kids going to be here the whole time? I thought your mama was keeping them while we were here in Vegas?"

"She had a doctor's appointment today, so she is coming here tomorrow to pick them up. But I know the drill GT; keep them far away from Elle as possible. You need to help me find a way to make sure she doesn't cave in and take the spot that should be mine," Raven stated.

Just when I was about to answer, Brooke walked in mad as hell. I was in her suite, so I could spend some time with my sons without Elle knowing about it. I made sure Brooke booked a full day of spa services for Elle, so she wouldn't leave the hotel room.

My sister knew all about me, Raven, and our kids. She helped me make sure that Elle never found out.

"Why are you stomping in here looking so pissed off, sis?"

"Doom broke things off with me because of the shit that happened at the studio! Now, he's fucking his damn secretary! If Elle would have just kept her damn mouth shut and danced, none of this shit would have happened!" Brooke raved as she slammed herself down in the chair.

I don't know why Brooke thought she and Doom were anything more than bed buddies, because he never took her out anywhere or claimed her. My sister always went after men in the industry that only saw her as a past time. They would dog her out, but she kept picking them over and over again. You would think she would have learned by now because just like me, Doom wasn't going to stop fucking other women and he shouldn't have to.

"Sis, I told you before that men with power won't settle for just one woman. Doom is damn near a billionaire and owns half the damn south. You need to cut your losses and accept that you will always have to share if you want to be with someone like Doom. If you can't accept it, then find you one of those square ass men to settle down with."

"Shut up, GT! Doom loves me, he just isn't ready to accept it yet. I'm too much of a strong woman for him to handle, and I scare him. I own my own management company and won't put up with his shit. I'm gorgeous, driven, and not afraid of expressing my sexuality. That's alright though, because soon, he will realize it was a mistake to let me go. Now, back to the problem at hand. If you don't want to lose Elle, I suggest you keep her away from Savior. Not only is he richer and finer than you, he can make her dreams come true," she replied.

I was about to tell her to mind her business when her words made me pause. Elle had always wanted to be a performer. Her mama had her in singing lessons and dance classes to make sure her daughter had all the skills to be well-rounded and become a star. Back when I met her, I was an insecure choir boy who was more worried about his grades. Somehow, I was lucky enough to catch the eye of the captain of the dance team and most popular girl in the school.

The older Elle got, the more beautiful and talented she became. That's when I told her I didn't want her to sing and steered her more toward dance. For one, the last thing I wanted was for her to make it and I didn't. Plus, I didn't want anyone else to have her. When I found out about the talent show, Brooke and I kept it from her because there was a good chance, she would have won instead of me. Once I won and my career started taking off, I threw her a bone and had her start choreographing my videos and performances. It also allowed me to have her in my sights when I went on tour. Elle would never cheat on me, but I didn't want to take any chances. After a while, her career took off just like mine and everyone wanted her to choreograph for them. I was the one who controlled which jobs she took, which was for mostly female clients. I thought she was content being one of the most sought-after choreographers in the industry, but apparently the sliver of hope to sing professionally was rearing its ugly head.

"Damn, I thought she was over this shit! I mean, she makes good money as a choreographer. Hell, she has been getting more bookings than Kiara lately, and that's saying something, since Kiara is at the top of her game. Plus, that hoe will do anything for gigs! Hell, I got her a few times, myself. Now you know if men were picking Elle over pussy and head, she must be good. I mean, I could press her more about killing Ivy, but I've already been doing that shit. Do you have something in mind, sis, or are you just talking?"

"Well, I do, but you might not like it. You know when it comes to your precious Elle, you don't like to do anything to tarnish her reputation. But that may be what's needed to keep her from outshining you and taking Raven's place on Saveon's album. Raven is the mother of your children, and she has to support them financially, GT. Don't get me wrong, I know you do your part, but your sons are accustomed to the finer things in life and Raven needs to make sure she can provide, in case you act dumb and decide to kick your real family to the curb," Brooke explained.

Raven started clapping and added, "Right, sis! Because the way he takes Elle's side over mine, it's only just a matter of time before he chooses her over me and his kids! I know what I signed up for when we started messing around, but that still doesn't mean I like being treated like I'm second best. You know how hard I have been trying to get Savior or Saveon to notice me, GT. Not only to work with, but to get them on my roster. My preference is Savior because he's not married, and I would hit the jackpot if I ended up as his wife. But being Saveon's mistress would keep my pockets fat, too because he would have to pay for my secrecy."

"Raven, you are family and everything, but I have to be

honest with you. Savior and Saveon are never going to fuck with you like that because of your reputation. Everyone in the industry knows how you get down. The Morrison brothers are selective on who they kick it with, and you are not it, boo. Kiara snuck in because she always plays that innocent girl role, when in fact, she's just another fame hungry hoe, who knows how to hide her true nature well. Hell, I should know because I manage her sneaky pussy ass! Now professionally, you might have a chance to work even more with them, but you need to stop acting so damn thirsty. Doom already did you a favor by getting Savior to work with you on your album. Now, if you are able to get him to put you on with his brother's new project, it will open you up to a whole new audience. Which means more money and opportunity, to skyrocket your career. However, you would have to dial down your hoeish ways, and we would have to make Elle's reputation worse than yours," Brooke explained.

Raven smiled, and I could tell my sister was on some good bullshit. I didn't like where this was headed at all.

"Hold up, Elle is tied to me, so if you fuck up her reputation then what will that do to me? Everyone knows she's my fiancé and a good woman. Hell, she barely leaves the house, so how can we catch her doing bad things when she ain't into that kind of shit?"

"We make her a part of our parties and catch the shit on tape. I mean, Big Tex is having a party tomorrow night, and we all planned to go. This time, you bring Ms. Perfect and have Tex seduce her and get it on camera," Brooke stated.

My blood boiled, and I punched the door. Elle was mine; I didn't want another man touching what belonged to me. Big

Tex was an ex-porn star and held exclusive sex parties around the world for celebrities and dignitaries. There usually was only around twenty guests exclusively invited and anything went on at the parties. You could fuck whoever you wanted, anyway you wanted. That's where I met Raven, and we conceived our sons. I brought Brooke last year, and she was just as hooked as I was. But never did I think about bringing Elle.

Biting the inside of my jaw, I growled, "You want me to take Elle to a fucking orgy and let big dick Tex fuck my fiancée and get that shit on tape? That's your fucking plan, Brooke? Well, let me tell you now, that's shit's not going to work! Elle's not going to just hop on the next dick!"

"Yes, that's exactly the plan! If she won't cooperate, GT, then we might have to give her a little something to relax her and let nature take its course. Raven and I both can attest that Tex will have her dripping and moaning so good, that she will give up that innocent act and spread her legs! Look, GT, it's time for you to let your past go and look toward your future. Raven is a superstar and the mother of your children. She has kept quiet for years and put up with your shit. Now, it's time to repay her loyalty and give her what she wants. Which is to expand her fanbase and record with the Morrison Brothers. Claim her and your children in public and make Elle look like a clinging bitch, who killed your baby. We can spin it and make it look like you stayed because she was mentally unstable. Sure, you had kids on her, but we can say your relationship has been over for years and you fell in love with Raven. Your fans already want Raven to be with you and not Elle, anyway. Let's face it, bruh, the bitch is basic and boring. You two together would be the *it* couple of R&B, and you're already blossoming career would skyrocket, GT. Look, I know you love Elle but, this is where you have wanted to be your whole life. Don't let Elle steal that away from you. She is never going to accept your lifestyle like Raven would. Raven knows you need to be free to fuck who you want, but ultimately, the choice is yours. Do you want Elle or your career?" Brooke questioned as she walked over to me, putting her arms around me.

Closing my eyes, I let her words flow through my mind. I thought about all the good times Elle and I had shared over the years. How she helped me grow not only as a singer but as a man. She had been down for the nerdy choirboy, Grant Wells, since middle school when no one knew who I was. The broke and always bullied young man, who used to get teased for not having the newest and best clothes. Elle wanted him even now, but I wasn't Grant anymore. In some ways, some of the hostility I had toward Elle, was because she reminded me of that weak ass little boy, I used to be. Grant Wells was dead and buried.

GT Wells was alive and well, as the Prince of R&B! No longer a nobody, but rich and famous beyond anything, I imagined growing up. Every man wanted to be me, and every woman wanted to be in my bed, but Elle didn't want GT or my new lifestyle. For the past few years, we had been arguing more, and I had to hide the lifestyle I loved because I knew she wouldn't accept it. Maybe I was holding on to something that had died a long time ago. Hell, I loved her, but I loved the fame more. Raven and I weren't a love match, but she loved her image and career just like me. Like Brooke said, she accepted me for who and what my new life entailed. With her, I could be free to do what I wanted, and she wouldn't expect shit in return. Hell, she loved the parties more than me, so we would have another shared interest. But the thing was, I still loved Elle and didn't want anyone else to have her. Call me selfish, but I was the first and only man to be inside of her. Then the guilt of letting her being taken advantage of was messing with me. Despite everything we had been through, Elle still had faith in me to keep her safe. How could I agree to violate her trust by drugging her and having a sex tape of her made for the public? Could I live with myself afterward?

Surprisingly, the answer shocked the fuck out of me once I went over everything Brooke and Raven had said to me.

"Okay, you're both right. Look, the plan is a go, but don't give her anything that will kill or hurt her. I might be fucking her over, but I don't want her dead or hurt either. Tell Big Tex to be gentle with her or I will make his life a living hell!"

Raven smiled, came over, and kissed me deeply. As always, my dick stood at attention when she touched me. When she pulled away, she said, "Thank you, baby. I promise you, our lives are going to be nothing but hot sex, diamonds, platinum records, and lots of money! But just to ease your mind, Big Tex would never do anything to her that she wouldn't want done. I know you love her GT, so as soon as she is in one of the bedrooms, I think you should leave. You don't need to be there when it happens. All you have to do tomorrow night is get Elle to the party and let Brooke and I take it from there."

Slowly, I nodded my head as Brooke and Raven started going over the plan for tomorrow night. I felt fucked up for what I was about to do to Elle because she had always had my back and loved me when I was just old Grant Wells. But I knew in my heart, our time was over. Grant was dead, and the new GT Wells needed to bury him for good. Which meant Elle was the only thing from my past that needed to go, in order for my career to rise. I would just have to get over my love for her and deal with the consequences of my actions later.

Sitting outside by the pool, I watched the workers getting everything ready for the crowd that I was sure was coming later. Luckily, Grant's guilt afforded me the option of being in the private VIP Cabana in the private oasis area away from everyone because I desperately needed my solitude. I thought the surroundings would offer me some clarity or peace from my problems, but unfortunately, my spirit and mind were still troubled.

For weeks, Grant had been pissed at me because he got kicked out of the studio. He accused me of everything from trying to sabotage his career, to wanting to fuck Savior for a record contract. Grant and Brooke both teamed up on calling me names and blaming me for some shit I had no control over. Even my own damn mama was putting her two cents in, on how I was supposed to handle the situation.

This Vegas trip was supposed to be our weddingmoon before we got married. We were supposed to be excited, happy, and ready to make love in every inch of our suite. Instead, just the thought of spending three weeks with him made me sick to my stomach. My mental was all the way fucked up right now, and I didn't know how much more I could take.

I had started seeing a therapist and was given medicine to help me with my depression and anxiety. The old me before I lost Ivy was starting to come back, and I was already thinking about making some changes in my life. Luckily, I had my own manager who had nothing to do with Brooke or Grant. Brooke had been heated when I chose JJ Barnes over her. But even then, I was starting to see changes in her I didn't like. I'm glad I followed my instincts because JJ had been a godsend! She was adjusting my schedule, so I could take some time off from choreographing. Too much shit was going on with me right now, and I needed to get my house in order. The shit I was putting up with before, was now starting to make me want to snap and beat the hell out of Brooke, Grant, and my mama's asses. To make matters worse, he invited my mama to come with us on our trip or should I say to make sure I stayed in line.

"Damn, Elle, you could have told me that you were coming out to the pool this morning! You could've called my room, and I would have met you down here. I guess, you call yourself being salty because I got on you about getting your man in trouble! Well, sorry not sorry! I didn't raise you to be stupid, Elle. Grant can take care of you, baby, if you just sit back and let him be a man! Who cares if he dips out every now and then? As long as he doesn't bring you back a disease or have a side chick's child, it shouldn't matter. As his wife, you will have his last name, live in a fancy mansion, and be the proud owner of his black card with full access to all his accounts. If he cheats then hit him where it hurts, his pockets!" my mama stated as she walked into the cabana.

Holding up my hand, I responded, "Nope, don't even bother sitting down, Mama. I came out here for some peace and quiet, so I could think some things through. The last thing I need is Grant's biggest fan out here trying to tell me I should accept him cheating on me and being disrespectful! As a matter of fact, why don't you go do what you do best and shop on Grant's dime. Just charge the shit to his room."

"Girl, who are you talking to like that! I'm your mama, and I'm supposed to tell you when you are fucking up! You are engaged to GT Wells, one of the biggest names in music out there right now. He gives you everything you want, but you still don't appreciate him! I mean, look at you, Elle. Your nails are basic, you aren't wearing makeup, and your hair is in a bushy ball on top your head! You should be rocking, fresh nails, straight or wavy bundles, your face should be beat to the Gods, and Lord knows you could stand a few ass injections and a titty job! No wonder he cheats with Instagram models! His fiancée is out here looking like Basic Betty next door!" she ranted.

Staring at her for a moment, I tried to calm myself down before I said something to my Mama that I might regret later on.

"Mama, you need to leave now! Do you hear how you are talking to me? I'm your daughter, and you should be the first one telling me to leave him because he's disrespecting me! The only reason you even like him is because of his money and status. Back when he was just Grant Wells, you couldn't stand him and wanted me to date the captain of the football team, Andre, because he was headed to the NFL. But what you fail to realize is that I make money and have my own status. People pay me big money to choreograph for them and one of the top producers in music wants me to be on an album. You should be proud of me and bragging on my accomplishments, as my mother. Despite not having a big ass and titties like the skanks Grant sleeps with, I am beautiful in my own right, Mama! If I have to alter myself in order to keep a man, I don't want him!"

"I am proud of you, Elle. But the little money you make isn't as much as what GT can give you. If you don't want to have surgery, fine! But the least you could do is get your hair pressed out, your nails done, and put some make-up on. That's all I'm asking before you lose everything, we worked so hard for!" she responded.

My mouth hung open as she spouted out the "we" word. This was too much! "You really don't give a damn about me, do you? All you care about is the money and lifestyle that Grant can give you. Mama, I lost my baby because of his cheating, and you blamed me for it! Not once did you give me one hug or wipe my tears, when I was breaking down from losing Ivy! For months, I was depressed and thinking about killing myself, just so I could be with my little girl! Did you not once think that I needed you? For you to come and wrap your arms around me and tell me everything was going to be alright?"

Mama froze at my words, and her face dropped. Grabbing

my hand, she looked at me and replied, "Elle, I'm sorry you feel that way. Never once did I mean to blame you for Ivy's death because I know how much you wanted and loved your baby. But you need to see it from my perspective as your mother. You think I am hard on you because I don't love you, but that's not true. I want the best for you because you are my daughter, and I don't want you to suffer like I did. If you think love is the only thing you need to be happy, then you are sadly mistaken. When your father died, all he left us with was eleven hundred dollars and an eviction notice. He promised me the world, but all I ended up with was a broken heart, debt, and promises never fulfilled. I don't want that same struggle for you, Elle. In life, there is no such thing as a perfect man. GT loves you baby and can give you the kind of life you deserve. If you have to tolerate turning a blind eye to a few groupies here or there, so what. Sometimes, it's the price we have to pay if we want it all. Now, I'm going to head back in and give you your space. I love you, Elle, more than anything in this world, even when you think I don't."

She placed a kiss on my cheek and walked off. I wanted to say more to her, but I knew no matter what I said, my mama wouldn't get it. It wasn't in her to understand that I would rather have love and respect over money any day!

"You know, if you keep biting your lips like that, you might chew them off," Savior stated, as he leaned around the corner from the neighboring cabana.

Jumping, I replied, "How long have you been over there? I didn't know you were staying here."

"Yeah, my crew is actually staying in the private villas.

They each have their own pools, but I had a meeting early this morning with the event coordinator about my afterparty for the Star Awards. Since it was so peaceful out here, I decided to stay and write some lyrics. I saw you walk up, but I didn't say anything because it looked as if you had a lot on your mind and needed the solace," he explained as he came around the cabana and sat down across from me.

Frowning, I questioned, "Since you have been there the whole time, does that mean you heard the conversation between my mama and me?"

"Yeah, unfortunately, I did. I'm sorry about your daughter's death, Elle. Believe me, I understand how much it hurts to lose a child. Not to mention, the guilt you feel for surviving and being here without them. I wish I could say it gets better, but the pain never gets easier. You just learn how to live with it and survive one day at a time. Now, your situation with your mama is something entirely different, but you definitely shouldn't listen to her advice. For one, you are gorgeous just the way you are. Two, you should do what makes you happy, Elle, money ain't everything," Savior stated.

I tried not to read too much into his compliment and ignore the butterflies in my stomach. Instead, my mind wandered to his words and the pain in his eyes when he mentioned losing loved ones. Everyone had heard the story about his wife and unborn child being murdered. There was no amount of "I'm sorry for your loss" that could fix his pain. Since I didn't know what to say to ease the pain in his eyes, I decided to open up to him about my own feelings. For some reason, Savior had a demeaner that made you want to open up to him. Plus, the fact that he was willing to listen--when the closest people to me didn't--made the decision to be open easier.

"To be honest with you, I have no clue what makes me happy anymore. It's been years since I have been truly happy with anything in my life, besides dancing and finding out I was pregnant with Ivy. My schedule hasn't allowed any time to even think about what would make me happy. This is the first time in month's my schedule has been free."

"Then how about you spend the day with me, and we could put our heads together to figure out what can make you smile again. I promise, I'm not trying to get into your pants either. It just seems like you need a friend right now, and I happen to have some free time today. There are some sights in Vegas we could explore to start things off, so are you down?" he asked.

Grant and my mama's voice's popped into my mind, already going off on me for even thinking about taking him up on his offer. But the old part of me flared up and said, "why the hell not!" Grant wasn't here, and there was no way I wanted to spend the day with my mama in the hotel room being lectured. What did I have to lose by spending the day away from my problems? "Alright, but don't try any funny shit because I do have mace! Let me grab my purse from the room, and we can head out."

"No need, pretty, I got you. It's not liked my pockets are hurting, and I did ask you to tag along. Let me just call Tese, so he and his girlfriend can come with us. He would kill me if I left the hotel by myself. My sister in law and brother just got in, so we might as well make it a party. Just give me a minute to call everybody and get the hotel to get us a bus to travel around in," he answered as he guided me toward the lobby.

As I stood waiting, in my mind, I knew that what I was doing would more than likely, start some shit. But just for once, Elle was going to do what she wanted and deal with the aftermath later.

I WAS STALKING THE FLOORS OF THE HOTEL, WAITING FOR any sign of Savior and his entourage. Earlier, I'd tried to bribe the clerk to tell me his room number, but the hoe wasn't budging on giving me the information. I was determined more than ever on making Savior come back to me.

It had taken me months to get Savior to see me as more than just a bed buddy, and I had fucked it up by releasing that video. I felt like he should have understood where I was coming from and given me another chance. We were both big names in the industry and our fans wanted to know about our relationship. So, I didn't see anything wrong with making videos of us.

Every other famous couple had YouTube channels and were all-over social media, being everyone's black love goals. Once we made it official, I just knew my fame was about to skyrocket more. Dancewear, make-up lines, and big-name brands would beg to be my sponsor. However, since he didn't want to coop- erate in the videos, we were being called boring, and I was losing followers. That's when I came up with the idea to make a sex tape and pretend it was an accident. I knew Savior would be upset, but I didn't think he would just throw away our relationship and treat me like I did him wrong! He had to understand we were a brand! For months, I had been trying to get him to take me back, but he wasn't budging.

Usually, I didn't let my feelings get involved. I had really fallen in love with Savior, and I was missing him like crazy. To top it off, my manager was telling me my viewership and my choreography requests were dropping. The artists who used to beat down my door to choreograph their videos and tours, were now flocking to that hoe, Elle! I had to do whatever it took keep my name out there.

I didn't know her personally, but I damn sure knew her fiancé. Before I met Savior, GT and I used to be lovers during his first tour. I was his choreographer and lead dancer back then. Brooke, my manager, hooked me up with the gig and told me her brother was interested in me. I thought GT and I could help each other out both professionally and personally. But soon, I found out I was just another number to him. After weeks of amazing sex while we were on the road, he dropped me in the middle of the tour and made his no-name girlfriend his new choreographer and lead.

Usually, I was picky with who I let in my bed, but GT caught me slipping. I tried to look for relationships that could benefit me and my career. I thought GT would be someone I could manipulate and take from his woman. Unfortunately, he played me after he got what he wanted. Luckily, he didn't spread any rumors about me, but to drop me in the middle of a tour, for his woman was fucking with my money and ego. Men had begged to be in my bed, and this asshole dumped me for a plain ass nobody! Ever since then, I hated to hear the name Elle Jamison.

My phone rang, and I rolled my eyes as I saw my manager, Brooke, was calling me. She was really starting to get on my fucking nerves.

"What is it now, Brooke? I told you, I am working on getting back together with Savior. You just have to give me more time."

"Don't get mad an attitude with me because he found out who you really are! I was just calling to tell you that I am working on something on my end to put you on top again. But in order to make sure it works, I need you to come to Big Tex's party tonight," Brooke stated.

Scowling down at my phone, I responded, "That's a big hell no! You and GT tricked me into going one time, and I told you it's not my scene."

"Well, if you want to get rid of your biggest competition, you will. Look, Kiara, I asked Big Tex to do a favor for me. He won't do it unless you agree to be his partner at one of his parties. I can't go into details, but if you do this one thing, then Elle will never steal another job from you again," she explained.

Big Tex had been sniffing around me for years, wanting to have sex with me, but there was no way in hell I was fucking a porn star. There was no telling how many women he had slept with, and I wasn't trying to catch something I couldn't get rid of. Brooke had lost her damn mind!

"Sorry, but not happening! I suggest you figure out something else, Brooke. Now, I have to go and try my own way of getting back on top, and it damn sure doesn't include climbing on top of Big Tex!

"Bitch, you are stupid as hell! It's not like you haven't fucked to get ahead in your career before! Now you need to—" Brooke started yelling before I hung up in her face.

I couldn't believe this bitch was asking me to fuck a porn star as a favor! If Brooke kept pushing me, I would just have to find a new manager! She was already on shaky ground because as my manager, Brooke should have been helping me advance my career, but lately, it felt as if she was neglecting my career and focusing more on her brother's.

"Savior, they said the bus should be pulling up in about five minutes. I'm going to grab the girls, so we can head out," I heard Matese, Savior's bodyguard say.

Matese couldn't stand me, and the feeling was mutual. I remember trying to get Savior to fire him, and he cussed me out. His bodyguard had been the reason I hadn't been able to get to my man. But this time, I was going to talk to Savior no matter what.

I got up from the sofa and peeked around the pole. Matese walked away from Savior, and I knew this was my time to get to my man. Pushing up my titties in the tight black bodycon dress and smoothing down my hair, I strutted over to Savior. He was into his phone, so he didn't see me approaching.

Smiling, I stated, "Savior, hey! I didn't know you were staying here. It's been a minute since we have seen each other, and I've missed you. If you aren't doing anything, how about we head to the bar and catch up!"

"Naw, that's alright, I already have plans. You can stop lying and acting like you just happened to be here. The front desk already informed my security team that there was a stalker or crazed fan trying to get to me. Tese said it was probably you, but I told him, you knew how I felt about you and wouldn't come near me again. Why are you here, Kiara?" he spat, in a rude tone.

Savior had always been a gentleman, and this new attitude was throwing me off. I knew he was upset, but this was not what I was expecting. "Baby, why are you talking to me like this? I get you are upset about the sex tape, but you have to know it was an accident. Now, I've given you time to calm down, and it's time for us to get back together. Our fans are asking for it, and we deserve to give our love a second chance. You know you miss me, Savior, because our feelings were strong for each other. Why are you acting like you don't care about me, when you used to be in my bed every night."

"Kiara, you're right, the bedroom was the one place I did care about, but now I don't. You think it was something deeper between us than what it was. We said we would give us a try, and that shit didn't work out. I can't lie and say I didn't care about you as a person, Kiara, but what we had wasn't love. It was more lust than anything. Like I told you then, there has only been one woman for me, and that was my wife. There is nothing between us, and you need to accept it," he stated, with a serious look on his face.

It felt like the air had been sucked out of my body. I thought Savior was moving on with me, and apparently, his feelings were never involved. My heart felt like he had snatched it out and stomped on it. Then, the overwhelming feeling of being used, played in my mind. I didn't like this feeling at all! Usually, I was the one getting everything I wanted, not the other way around.

"So, basically you are telling me, you used me as a living sex doll! Someone to fuck and suck, but not to build with or love. What about my feelings, Savior? Did you even think about those when you were using me?"

"You can stop playing the victim, Kiara, because we both know we weren't going to make it together. Did we have good times, yes. But the bad outweighed the good. Now, what I want you to do is stop stalking me and move on with your life. There are plenty of other rappers, athletes, or actors who would love to have you on their arm and be a part of your social media world; unfortunately, I'm not one of them," Savior countered.

"Hey, Savior, Matese said the bus is out front, now," Elle stated, walking up to Savior.

My mouth dropped as yet again, this bitch popped up in my way! "What the fuck are you doing here with my man? Does your fiancée know you are fucking around on him?"

"Don't answer that, Elle. Why don't you go ahead and get on the bus, and I will join you in a minute," he told her, with a smile on his face.

Elle smiled back and replied, "Alright, I will. Sorry, if I caused any trouble."

"Naw, you alright. She doesn't have a say so, on who I hang with. Tell everybody I'm on the way," Savior responded.

This bitch had the nerve to look at me with pity as she walked by. The innocent look on her face didn't fool me one damn bit! This hoe was trying to take my place in my man's bed!

It was bad enough she was stealing my clients and sponsors and her fiancé chose her over me. But now Savior was sniffing after her ass too!

As soon as she went out the door, I snapped! "So, to get back at me, you decided to find the basic ass version of me, huh? Are you trying to embarrass me by being with her? At least if you are going to replace me with someone who is an upgrade because Elle is definitely not on my level!"

"Damn, just when I thought your attitude couldn't get any worse. You are calling her basic, but you are just like the rest of these women on Instagram bent over in your draws, getting your ass and lips injected, and bragging about your fake ass relationship. That's being basic. Elle doesn't try to be anything but who she is. There's something special in her that people see, which is why she is gaining more clients than you are, and people want to be around her. I'm sure that is making you insecure as hell because you don't have anything special to offer. Now, I have to go, and this will be the last time we are going to have this conversation. Next time, I'm going to take my sister-in-law's advice and file a restraining order. Goodbye, Kiara," he threatened before walking off.

"You heard what my brother said, Kiara. Why won't you leave him alone, after everything that you did to him," his sister-in-law, Pepper, asked as she walked up.

I couldn't stand her ass because she was always blocking me like Matese. My mood was already fucked-up because Savior had embarrassed the hell out of me. Now, he was standing outside, laughing at something Elle's fake ass was saying. He might have thought he had the last word, but he and Ms. Elle had another thing coming.

"Mind your business, Pepper, and we won't have a problem."

"Oh, we already have one, Kiara, and if you keep messing with Savior, we are going to have an even bigger one. Security, make sure she leaves the premises and isn't allowed back in until my client checks out," Pepper ordered, to two burly hotel security officers.

They grabbed my arms and replied, before dragging me through the lobby, "Yes ma'am, we will take care of it."

"What the hell! Do you know who I am? Let me go!" I screamed as they continued dragging me toward the side of the lobby.

Pepper was smiling, and I noticed at least twenty people recording me get tossed out of the hotel. It dawned on me that my followers, the blogs, and haters would all be laughing at me in a matter of minutes. I had to get the hell out of here fast while I still had some dignity left. My mind was going over what to say, so I could spin this shit in my favor.

Finally, I yelled, "Tell Savior he can't keep dodging me and his baby! Y'all see them manhandling me, and I'm pregnant! Yeah, get this on tape, so everyone can know what a deadbeat the almighty Savior Morrison is and how he treats the mother of his child!"

An older lady in the crowd shouted, "Kiara is pregnant with Savior's baby! I told you she was getting thicker! I'm calling the police because y'all are going to make her lose her baby! Savior should be ashamed of himself!"

Pepper stood there with her mouth open and shaking her head. That's what her ass got for trying to fuck with me! The guards immediately let me go and more cameras were pulled out and aimed in my direction. I was so happy that my make-up and hair stylist had gotten me straight before I left my room this morning. The bodycon dress I was wearing was hugging my curves and enhancing my stomach that was still a little bloated from my cycle just ending.

Rubbing my stomach, I cued up my tears and yelled, "Tell Savior I still love him, but he has to start treating me better. All I want is for us to be a family! I'll leave for now, but I'll be back soon, so we can talk about the baby."

Pepper was so pissed off, she turned and stomped off in the direction of the bus. The crowd shook their heads and gave me congratulations on the baby while expressing how Savior wasn't shit. I milked my little performance for all it was worth, hoping for a new headline and more followers.

After taking a few pictures with some new fans, I headed outside and got in my waiting limo. Pulling out my phone, I dialed Brooke and said, "Fine, tell him I'm in. But you better have something good for that bitch, Elle, because she has me fucked-up!"

"I'm glad you came to your senses, and hell yes, I have something real good for Elle. You need to tell me what changed your mind. But first, let me say, bravo, bitch. You are trending every damn where right now! Why didn't you tell me you were pregnant by Savior? We could have made a lot of money leaking it to the press," Brooke questioned.

Waving the driver to pull off, I replied, "You know damn

well, I'm not pregnant! I don't even like kids and don't plan on having any. Savior embarrassed the hell out of me, and I needed to change the narrative for the cameras. But please tell me why your ugly ass sister-in-law was all over my man!

"Elle was with Savior? Damn, see, I told GT he wasn't going to give up on her! Look, Savior isn't trying to fuck her, Kiara. He wants her to sing on his brother's record, but that's not going to happen if I have anything to do with it. Just hold up your end of the bargain with Big Tex, and I will take care of the rest. Now, I'm just curious how you are going to keep up this pregnancy charade when you aren't pregnant," she inquired.

Biting my lip, I wondered that myself. Guess that was a bridge I would have to cross later on.

"Damn, she sings, too! Well, I guess that explains why he's even giving her the time of day. He eats, breathes, and sleeps music, so he will do anything to make that duet happen. I feel better now, because it didn't make any sense at all to me that Savior would want Elle instead of me. As far as the pregnancy, I don't know yet, Brooke. But one thing I do know is that I can milk this fake baby for the time being. Now, when am I supposed to meet up with Tex?"

"He is expecting you to have lunch with him this afternoon at Kabuto's," she answered.

Sighing, I responded, "Fine, but I'm not fucking him, Brooke, so you need to let him know that upfront."

"Kiara, now stop acting all bougie and shit because we need him to be compliant for what we have planned for Elle. Which means you are going to have to pry open those legs and give his ass a taste. It's not like you won't enjoy it because I know from experience that his big dick ass can fuck you into a coma. So, bitch you better hop on it, turn that man out, and get yours in the process. You will be killing two birds with one stone. Now, I have to go and get some shit ready for my little plan. Remember, we need Tex to make Elle pay," Brooke added.

I was about to ask her what she was up to because an uneasy feeling came over me at her words. Elle was definitely a thorn in my side, but that didn't mean I wanted to be a part of some shady shit that would land me in jail.

But before I could ask, we passed the Fountains at the Bellagio when I saw Savior. Pepper was taking a picture of him and Elle together, in front of the water. All thoughts of morality went out the window.

Whatever happened to Elle was just her karma for trying to be me. The one who would pay the most was Savior; he thought he could play with me and then toss me aside, just because he was a little camera shy. Either he was going to get with the program, or I was going to drag his name for the masses, every chance I got. Soon, he would come to his senses and realize that we were meant to be, both personally and professionally. Until then, I was going to do everything in my power to make his life a living hell. First, I needed to come up with a plan, to make this fake pregnancy a reality. Then, I was going to make sure there was no competition-- personally and professionally--for me. So, I resigned myself to the fact I was going to have to pull the gloves off, to get what I wanted the most.

Closing my eyes, I reluctantly said, "Alright, I'll fuck him. But you are going to tell me everything you plan on doing to that bitch, Elle. I want to make sure she isn't a problem."

"Girl, I got you. Now, are you sitting down?"

Rolling my eyes, I answered, "Yeah, now talk."

When Brooke finished telling me their plan, I smiled. It was fucked up but brilliant at the same time. I was glad I was on their side because these mutherfuckers were ruthless. It also gave me an idea on how to make my pregnancy a reality.

By the time I got finished with Savior, he would be begging me to be his wife.

"Have you decided when and how you are going to pop the question to Catrina?" my sister, Mashelle, asked as she gazed at the four-karat, heart-shaped engagement ring.

Taking the box from her, I closed it, put it back in my pocket, and answered, "I don't know yet, but it has to be the perfect time. She has been having it rough lately, with throwing up every five minutes. My baby is really putting her through it."

"I know, Trina looked horrible when she opened the door to your room earlier. I'm sorry, she couldn't go on the tour. But I am glad you decided to hang back at the hotel with me and have a brother-sister lunch. You've been away with Savior so much, I forgot what you looked like," she joked.

Laughing with her, I said, "Sorry, sis, you know I've been working hard. But enough about me. How are my niece and nephew doing?"

"Zen and Diamond are both thriving. You know Zen is walking and getting into everything with his cute bad butt.

Diamond loves being in school, cheerleading, and dance. Especially with Bree and Kevin being there. She still has nightmares, but counseling is helping her. The only other thing she talks about is her Uncle Tese and all the stuff he keeps sending her every week. You and Jace need to stop spoiling her so much," Mashelle answered.

My sister had officially adopted Diamond not too long ago, and Jace was in the process of surprising her with adoption papers for Zen. They might not be biologically her children, but you would never guess it by the way she loved and cared for them. When my sister told me she had cancer, my heart dropped. My sister was my everything, and I didn't want to lose her because we were all we had. I thanked the Lord above for keeping her here with us.

"Hey, my niece and nephew can have anything their heart desires. How are you and Jace doing? I'm surprised he's not here, making sure none of these singers or rappers steal his girlfriend.

My sister flinched when I said the word girlfriend, and I knew something was up. Jace was my boy, but if he was doing my sister dirty, we were about to have a problem.

Mashelle responded, "We are alright, I guess. He is out at a meeting with one of his suppliers right now, but should be back here at the hotel soon. Look, honestly, I'm not sure if we are alright or not. We do all the things a couple would do, but we are still living in separate households, and there's no ring on my finger. You know how much I love him and our kids, Tese. I've never wanted to be anybody's baby mama, and he's still fucked-up from how his ex-wife betrayed him. Believe me, I've given him time, but it's been over a year now and something has to give. Last week, we had my eggs and his sperm joined together, so we can have a baby via surrogate. How does that look for us to be having a third child together and no plans for the future?"

"Damn, sis, I don't know what to say. On one hand, congratulations on the baby because I know how much you have wanted a big family. I'm happy as hell that you are getting the family you deserve. But on the other, you need to talk to Jace and tell him how you feel, Shelle. Don't be afraid to ask for what you want or deserve. Hell, you have never been one to bite your tongue with everyone else, so don't let your fear of losing him keep you silent now. Catrina told me what she wanted, and I knew if I didn't step up and get over what Janiyah did to me, I would lose her. It took me a minute to get myself together and realize she was nothing like Janiyah, and my heart would be safe with her. Bottom line is, stop being scared of losing him before you lose yourself, Shelle."

Smiling, she replied, "Look at my little Matese giving me advice! Not to mention, about to settle down and start a family! I am so proud of you and can't wait for Catrina to have my first niece or nephew! Well, besides my Kevin, Bree, and Killian, who are my hearts! But it's different when it's the boy you used to change diapers for, becomes a man. Mama and Daddy would be proud of you, Tese."

"I don't know about all that, sis. But thank you for the compliment. Look, sis, there's something I need to talk to you about. I ran into someone at the hospital and found out some shit that blew my damn mind."

Mashelle frowned, but I noticed she wasn't looking at me.

When her face turned red, I knew my sister was about to snap on someone. "What is that bitch doing here? That's okay because I owe her an ass whooping anyway!"

"Damn, sis, who are you about to fight?"

Shelle scoffed as she stood up and responded, "Your ex, that's who! What the fuck is she doing in Vegas anyway? You know what, it doesn't even matter. She and her ugly ass boyfriend can catch these hands!"

Turning around, I saw Janiyah with her daughter on her hip and Maurice was holding her hand with a blank look on his face. I was shocked she was standing here after I had searched for them since the day after I saw her at the hospital.

"Wait, Shelle, don't touch her. The kids are here, and I need to talk to her. Do you think you can watch out for me in case Catrina comes downstairs?"

Mashelle looked at me, shook her head in disgust and replied, "Please, tell me you aren't cheating on Trina with this bitch! You can't be that dumb to throw away someone who loves you, for the chick who fucked your best friend while you were locked down! Damn that, I'm going to beat your ass myself for thinking with your dick and not your head."

"I don't want any trouble, Mashelle. The last thing I came here to do is cause trouble in his relationship. We are not having an affair or whatever it is you think we are doing, but I just came here to talk to Matese about our son," Janiyah interjected.

My sister's head snapped around, and she said, "Son! Oh, hell naw! Matese, what the hell is she talking about?"

"Don't look at me like that, Shelle. I just found out I could possibly have a son about a month ago. I saw Janiyah at the hospital, then she got ghost before I could get a DNA test or ask her why she kept my son away from me."

Mashelle stared at me and took in everything I said. Finally, she said, "Fine, I believe you, Tese. This bitch has a habit of keeping secrets, so it doesn't even shock me that she would hide your son from you. But best believe Janiyah, my brother is getting a DNA test. Now, let's take this conversation to my room because the world doesn't need to hear this."

We all headed to Shelle's villa. I was nervous as hell when we got to the villas because Mashelle's was right next door to mine and Catrina's. Once we were inside, Janiyah laid her now sleeping daughter down on the couch. Maurice sat down beside her and stared at the TV, Mashelle had just turned on. Then she motioned for Janiyah and me to step out on the patio by the pool. It was perfect because we could still see the kids but had some privacy.

As soon as the glass door was closed, I turned to Janiyah and asked, "So, is he really mine, Janiyah, or are you playing games?"

"He's yours, Matese, I promise. There were a lot of times I wanted to tell you about him, but I couldn't. You don't understand what I have been through since you've been in jail. I know you think I betrayed you with Yo, but I didn't. He blackmailed me into being with him and wouldn't let me contact you. Last night, I left him and he's going to come after me and the kids. We need your help, or he's going to kill us."

Before I could respond, Shelle said, "So, you conveniently brought your ass out here playing damsel in distress. Nope, bitch, you aren't slick, and I'm not going to let you come here and fuck up what my brother has. Now, I can make a few calls and get you and your kids an Airbnb while we wait on DNA results. Tese can have some of his security guards outside so nothing happens to you. Other than that, all contact needs to come through me. I don't trust you not to cry your way onto my brother's dick."

"Look, I didn't come here to talk to you, Mashelle. This is between Matese and I because we were the ones who created Maurice. I don't remember you being there when we were fucking, so why do you think you have a say so in what we do with our child now!"

Mashelle was about to swing, so I jumped in between them and said, "Naw, both of you are doing too damn much! Janiyah, my sister has every right to not trust you because I know, I don't. If you really wanted me to know my son, you would have found a way to tell me before now. Sis, I'm not a child anymore. Let me handle this because it's my mess, and the last thing I need Maurice seeing is you fighting his mama. If he is mine, you are his auntie, and I don't want him to have a bad impression of you before he gets a chance to know you. Now, we are all grown and can come up with a solution other than fighting. First thing we need to worry about is getting the DNA test to see if he is my son."

"Yes, I think you definitely need to get a DNA test to see if our unborn child has a big brother or not! Or was this going to continue to be a big secret that everyone knew about except for me!" Catrina shouted as she stood across from us on our villa patio.

I should have known the yelling was going to draw Trina's attention; she was a light sleeper. Her blonde hair was in a messy ponytail, and she was wearing one of my t-shirts and a pair of leggings. Trina's eyes was red and had tears streaming down her face. The look of betrayal and hurt as she looked at me, tore me up. This was not the way I wanted her to find out. Especially on the trip where I planned to ask her to be my wife. Walking over to her, I stopped when she held her hand up and shook her head.

"Trina, please just let me talk to you for a minute. Look, I just found out last month that she had a child that could be mine. It was the night we found out we were going to have our baby. Janiyah and Maurice were at the hospital, and I ran into them. When I found out he was her son, I did the math and realized Maurice could be mine. Just when I was about to confront her, you called me. By the time I turned around, they were gone. I started searching for her, but she had moved, and I couldn't find them until Janiyah popped up here today. The reason I didn't tell you was because I wanted to get a DNA test first before bringing it to you."

Trina shook her head as she wiped her tears and replied, "That's not good enough, Matese! You should have told me that night about her and your possible son! If one of us has a problem, then we both do. I could have helped you find her because she is always at the hospital. When I saw her name was Janiyah, I didn't put two and two together and realize she was your ex. I could—"

"Excuse me, but I don't need you telling my business! You aren't supposed to anyway, right? Look, like I told Mashelle I'm only here because Maurice needs to know his father, and we are in danger. Now, I don't mind taking a DNA test to settle my son's paternity. I can pay for my own hotel room, and you all are welcome to come and get to know Maurice. But I do need to talk to Matese alone. It's a matter of life and death."

Mashelle responded, "If you don't have anything to hide or trying to steal dick, then why do you need to talk to him alone? Naw, that's alright, you can say what you need to say to him right now in front of me and his girlfriend."

"No, Mashelle, she can talk to him in private. If Maurice is his son, then there will be times I won't be around. If I can't trust him alone with her and he fucks up, then he wasn't the man for me to begin with. My head hurts, and I'm going to go and lay down. As a matter of fact, we have an extra room here. If they are in danger and that's your son, Tese, he is safer here with you and Mashelle next door. Plus, you need to get to know your son, and you can't do that at a distance. I have an old colleague who moved out here last year. They can come and do the DNA test and rush the results. But let me be clear, Janiyah. The only reason I am not beating your ass is because I'm pregnant and don't want to lose my child. Plus, if Maurice is Matese's son, we all need to be able to co-exist. I won't tolerate no baby mama bullshit in our lives. Notice the "Our" part sweetheart and remember that! You fucked up and he belongs to me now, and you can't have him back. Don't let the nice sweetness fool you because it can go sour real quick. Matese, all I have to say is don't try me. Unlike other people, I will walk out the door and won't come back if you fuck up. Mashelle, can you come and help me get the room ready for them?"

My sister answered, "Naw, Maurice can come and stay with you two, but Janiyah is going to stay here with Jace and me. Sis, you might be trusting and shit, but I am not! Her staying with you two is a Lifetime movie in the making. You don't need that type of stress on you right now."

I walked over to Trina just as she stepped into the villa and wrapped her in my arms. I bent and whispered in her ear, "Baby, can I at least have a hug before you go in? You don't have anything to worry about because I love you. I'd never hurt you like that, and you know it. Once we find out the DNA results, we can figure out what to do. Then it will be all about us the rest of the trip. Now, what was she trying to keep you from telling?"

Trina shook her head and answered, "Matese, I can't tell you that because not only can I lose my job and license, but it's her story to tell, not mine. I'm sure there are a lot of things she has to say to you, judging by her tracking you down."

"Fuck her! I don't owe Janiyah shit! If it ain't about Maurice, then fuck her!"

"Tese, I love you, but this is the unfinished business that I was afraid of popping up in our lives. You need to finish it, before we move on because I refuse to be a part of some back and forth shit. I deserve a man who is going to be all about me and no one else. So, if you still have feelings for her and they are stronger than the ones you have for me, tell me so I can move on. I have no problems co-parenting. Now, go and figure out what and who you want, just remember once you have made your choice, there's no coming back."

The look in her eyes said it all. She had already left me once before, and I didn't want a repeat. Catrina wasn't one for giving a lot of chances, and I didn't want to lose her either. "Alright, but I'm serious, Trina. I only want you. Go ahead and lay down, so my daughter can get some rest."

"Um hm, yeah we both know it's a boy. But good try, trying to change the subject."

She headed into the bedroom as my sister was coming in. Mashelle stared at me with disapproval in her eyes, and I couldn't even blame her. The whole situation was fucked up, and I knew it.

"Matese, don't fall for Janiyah's whoa as me story. I'm not doubting that Yo blackmailed her because he always was envious of you, but that was your boy, so I left it alone. But there were numerous times and people she could have reached out to for help, but she didn't. That bitch got hoodoo on you; you better watch your back!"

"Shelle, what the hell are you talking about?"

She replied, "How is it that she pops up at the hospital on the same day with your secret love child, just as your current girlfriend finds out she's pregnant? Then when you are about to propose to Catrina, here she comes to fuck that up too. The bitch ain't psychic, so I think she laced her pussy with some herb's and shit to track your ass down when you are happy. You need to wash your dick off with holy water."

I almost busted a lung from hearing that crazy ass shit, then countered, "Sis, you need to stop hanging around Kut's crazy ass. That sounds like some shit that she would say."

"It's the truth though. I'm going to have my best tracer in Nashville find out what is going on with Yo. I have a feeling she didn't tell us the whole story. Of course, when you have your little talk with her, see what you can find out. Just don't follow that urge to zombie voodoo walk your ass into some old pussy. Now, let me go in there and make sure my niece or nephew stays in there and bakes. I love you, Tese."

Shaking my head and opening the door, I answered, "I love you too, sis."

When I got outside, Janiyah was sitting at the patio table, biting her fingernails and looking inside at Maurice. I sat down opposite her and watched as my possible son stared blankly at the television.

"What's wrong with him, Janiyah? When I first met him, he was talking my head off. Now, he's quiet and lifeless."

Tears ran down her face as she answered, "He's been through hell, Tese, and it's all my fault. I hate to say it, but your sister is right. I should have never given into Yo's blackmail and told you or Mashelle about Maurice. Yo never hit Maurice, but he verbally abused him every chance he got because he was your son."

"Why did you let him, Janiyah? You are his mother and supposed to protect him from everything. At the least, you could have dropped him off to Mashelle, and she would have taken care of him until I got out of jail. I still don't understand how a man, I treated like my brother, suddenly flips the script and blackmails my girl. Make it make sense, Janiyah."

She wiped her tears and responded, "I don't know all of his reasons, Tese, but what I can say is that he was jealous of everything you had. Yo is crazy and vindictive, so who knows really what is going on in his head. But he knows what you did, Tese, when we were in high school. I don't know how he found out, but he has the gun and something else to prove it. He confronted me the last day I came to visit you. It was the day you paid the guard for us to have alone time, and we conceived Maurice that day."

I sat there in shock, trying to figure out how Yo knew about my first murder. Since it was my first time pulling the trigger, I wasn't exactly careful. Hell, I was scared shitless because the shit was unexpected and in my haste to getaway, I tossed the gun in an abandoned building.

"Fuck! He had to be following us that day. Unless, you told somebody else what happened, Janiyah!"

Scoffing, she responded, "Why would I tell someone that I was an accessory to murder, Tese! You aren't the only one he has hemmed up here, and you damn sure haven't had to endure the years of abuse and being basically raped every night, just so you could keep the man you love from being put to death by lethal injection. I had to find out where Yo hid the evidence! I've been through hell and back, losing my self-respect, my body, and now the man I love. So, don't act like I'm completely the bad guy in this situation!"

I closed my eyes and took a deep breath. There was no comeback to her about what she had to endure these past years because of me. I wanted to put all the blame on her because she hurt me to my core. But after hearing her out, I realized I played a big part in what happened between us.

"I'm sorry, Janiyah. Believe me if I had known he was using that against you, I would have gladly done the time for you and Maurice to be happy. You and the kids won't ever have to worry about being safe and cared for again. We can hook you up with a place to stay, and I can help you find a job once we get back to

Nashville. If you don't want to work, that's fine too because I will put money in an account for you and my son to live comfortably."

Janiyah responded, "Thank you, but I can take care of myself and my kids. I didn't find you for money, Matese. It was just time for you to get to know your son and for you to know the whole truth. I found out that Yo has a storage unit he has had ever since the day you went to prison. One night, I followed him there and saw him go inside one, and there was a big safe inside."

"Good give me the location and number of the unit, and I will have a friend of mine go there now and see if he can't get the evidence out. Then, I'll get him to check and see what's going on with Yo. Hell, knowing my sister, she probably already has someone checking on Yo as we speak. So, don't worry about anything and just chill. Did you tell Maurice I'm his father?"

She nodded and answered, "Yes, he knows who you are and that it's not your fault you weren't around. Our son is smart and such a good child. He is always looking out for his little sister, and they have the best relationship. To me, Maurice has the best parts of both of us, and I'm glad you are going to get the chance to know him. I guess, I should congratulate you on your new baby on the way. You must really love Catrina if you are expecting a child together."

Looking at Janiyah, I saw the pain and jealousy in her eyes. My heart hurt at being the one who caused it. She had been such a big part of my life since we were kids, and those memories, feelings of loyalty, and love didn't just go away. This was the woman I thought I would marry and have children with. It would be so simple to just let the past go and pick up where we left off. I couldn't because I was also in love with Catrina. It killed me that she had been right about me having unfinished business. Now, I was stuck in the house with the two women who shared my heart. I owed Janiyah the truth because despite my feelings for her, our time had passed.

"Yeah, I love her very much, and she's having my baby. I plan on making her my wife one day soon. Catrina is my future, Janiyah, and nothing or no one is going to change that. So, if you are here to cause trouble or have any hopes of us getting back together, you can forget it now. That woman inside has been with me through thick and thin, and I would never hurt her."

Tears fell from her eyes and she replied, "So, what about me, Matese? Don't you love me anymore? You act like what I've done to protect you wasn't shit! We have a child together who needs his family! I know, I said I didn't want to break up your happy home, but I thought you would at least think about giving us another try!"

"Janiyah, I will always love you, but what the fuck do you expect me to do? Drop the woman I love while she's pregnant, to give my ex who I don't fully trust, a try? I can't do that, and I won't. Look, you will find someone else and move on with your life. I'm about to head inside and see how Catrina is doing. Then, I'm going to spend some time with our son and get to know him."

As I stood up to leave, Janiyah got up and grabbed me with tears in her eyes. Then said the words that would stick with me forever. "That's the thing, I don't have a future, Matese. I'm dying."

Kiara really had me fucked up if she thought I would take her ass back. Now she was on some stalking shit, I didn't like it one damn bit.

"Um, if this is what you call cheering me up, then I can head back up to my room," Elle teased.

"Sorry about that, Elle. I was lost in thought for a minute. I promised you a good time, and I intend to keep my promise. So, how did you like the fountain show?"

She laughed and said, "It was gorgeous and over five minutes ago. Your brother and Pepper just went to go and get us all something to drink. They tried to ask what you wanted, but you've been in a trance with that mean mug on your face. Kiara really got to you, huh? I can tell she's a handful."

"Handful isn't the word that comes to mind when it comes to my ex. Kiara just can't seem to take no for an answer, and I'm tired of her popping up everywhere I go. Our relationship started out okay but ended up toxic as hell. But I guess, you know all about that yourself."

She flinched, and I felt bad about bringing up her and GT's relationship. I knew my relationship was a fucking joke, but she was still coming to terms with hers.

"Look, I'm sorry, Elle. I shouldn't have brought up your relationship when it's not my business."

She walked over to the rail and stared out at the water. The sun was highlighting her chocolate skin and the mass of curls gathered on top of her hair were blowing in the warm breeze.

Finally, Elle said, "It's alright, you didn't say anything that isn't the truth. I'm just in my feelings because GT isn't the man I fell in love with. I'm just coming to terms with it now, and it's hard to believe."

"Listen, this love shit ain't easy and anybody that says it is ain't never had it before. When it's not right though, you know it, but letting go of it is hard, period. After I lost my wife, Lake, I didn't want to accept it. Hell, there are still days it's hard to not think about losing her. She was my rib and our love was pure. Shit wasn't perfect but it made you want to work for it. It took me a long time to even entertain anything permanent. Now don't get me wrong, I was out here wilding out but nothing serious. When Kiara came around, I think it was more about me showing people I was ready to move on than really wanting a relationship with her. But I made the biggest mistake when I decided to put effort into our situationship, to see where it led to. I tried to force some shit that wasn't meant to be. When Kiara started showing her ass, it solidified she wasn't the one for me."

I leaned against the railing and was shocked when Elle grabbed my hand and started rubbing it. When I looked into her eyes, there was compassion and pain in their brown depths. Everything about Elle screamed good hearted, and GT was a fucking fool for not knowing what he had.

"I know, I've said it before, but I am really sorry about your wife. Losing Ivy about killed me, so I can't even imagine the pain you experienced losing them both at the same time. You are so strong, though; look at you living your life and making her proud as she watches over you. Believe me, I've just been existing since I lost Ivy and staying in a relationship that died a long time ago. I'm trying to get to the point you are now. I want to be happy and thriving, not just existing and accepting bullshit."

Placing my hand on hers, I asked, "Well, saying it's bullshit is the first step, Elle. Now, I see Saveon and Pepper headed our way. Judging by how fast they are walking and the amount of people with cameras in their hands, I think it's time for us to move on to the next attraction."

"I'm game! Where are we headed next?"

Laughing as she broke into a smile and jumped up and down like a little kid, I responded, "Madame Tussaud's to take some cheesy ass photos with wax figures. Let's head to the bus before we are on TMZ.

Once Elle and I made it to the bus, we looked out and the bodyguards had Pepper, and she was almost to the bus. My brother, however, was surrounded by a rowdy group of older church ladies who were smothering him with kisses and getting their fans signed.

Pepper got on the bus and was laughing her ass off. "I had to get the hell out of there, when one of those lovely little church ladies threw her granny panties in Saveon's face! I know it's wrong to laugh, but that was funny as hell!"

We all joined her as we saw the offending panties on the ground at Saveon's feet. Frank, one of Saveon's bodyguards, was finally able to steer my brother back to the bus and away from the ladies. Once he was on, we pulled off and headed down the strip to our next destination.

"Damn, Pepper, I thought you was supposed to have my back! They were trying to take me back to their bus."

Pepper shook her head and replied, "I'm sorry, baby, but you know the rule is to respect your elders."

"Alright, I see how it is. Don't be surprised when someone from the mother's board steals me away either."

By the time we pulled up to Madame Tussaud's, our sides were hurting from laughing at Pepper and Saveon acting a fool. Elle and Pepper had hit it off and walked off the bus, chatting away.

Saveon clapped me on the back as we were getting ready to get off the bus and join them, and said, "It's good to see you enjoying yourself, Save. But I have to ask, are you trying to get her into the studio or your bedroom?"

"Naw, nothing like that. Of course, I would love for her to join you on your record and on my label, but she's going through some things right now and needed a pick me up. GT is a fucking fool, and Elle is finally understanding that she deserves better."

Saveon smiled and replied, "You sure better doesn't mean

you, Save? I mean, you are single, and she's a good look for you. We've known her a few years, and Elle has never been anything but nice and drama free. She's gorgeous, and I know you have been peeping that because I saw you eyeing her ass as she got on the bus earlier."

"Come on, Saveon. I'm a man, and she has on leggings. Hell yeah, I looked! It doesn't mean I'm about to try and take advantage of her while she is vulnerable. Elle lost her baby, and she's still healing from that. Everyone around her is out for themselves, from what I overheard, and she needs someone in her corner. I know the kind of pain she is dealing with, and I just want to help her, the way you and Pepper helped me."

He nodded. "That's what's up. Well, Pepper likes her, and we both know she doesn't like everybody, so she has one more person on her side. I'm surprised with all the rumors and paternity lawsuits; Elle hasn't left him sooner. I admire her loyalty, but I've had personal experience with trying to hang on to a toxic person, and I would hate for her to have to go through the shit I went through. So, I will look out for her too. As a matter of fact, my dancer backed out on my performance at the Star Awards. Do you think Elle can fill in for her?"

"I don't know, but I'll ask. You know she is probably scheduled to dance for GT, but you might be able to sway her to do both."

He nodded, and we headed out and were immediately escorted in. Saveon and Pepper went one way, and Elle and I went another. We both used the phones on our camera to take pics of each other with different wax celebrities. She was goofy as hell and had me cracking up as she twerked on the wax statue of Beyoncé.

"Yo, I didn't know you swung that way."

"That's Bey, hell, I would switch over for a night with her!"

I laughed, and said, "Yeah, okay one night. Your ass would be turned out and swearing off dick after that."

"Nope, I love dick too much for that."

My dick jumped at her words, and I knew it was time to move on from this conversation. I walked away and she followed along.

"Let's head over to The Hangover Bar, so we can grab something to drink and wait on Pepper and Saveon."

Once she agreed, I asked, "So, Ms. Elle, how did you get into dancing?"

"Believe it or not, by watching Dirty Dancing, Fighting Temptations, and Sister Act 2 when I was younger. I loved the dancing and singing from all of those movies, then started doing it all over the house. My mama said she saw how talented I was, then started putting me in singing lessons, dance classes, and talent shows. My dream was to be the total package, singing, dancing, then maybe even acting. Hence, my obsession with Beyoncé."

Smiling, I asked, "Damn, I would pay to see some of those old dance photos or a video of some of your earlier performances. What made you stop singing? I mean, from what I heard in the dance studio, you have some real talent."

"Well, Grant was against me being in the music industry because he thought I would be taken advantage of by someone. Then we made plans to open up a performance arts school, where he did vocal lessons, and I would teach dance to kids and adults in our community. But that all changed when Grant won the talent contest that launched his career. He asked me to support him by choreographing his tour and singing wasn't on my radar anymore."

We made it to the bar and had a seat. I ordered a Hennessey while she ordered the Royal Flush. It was a nice vibe and once we got our drinks, I continued getting to know Elle more.

"Do you miss it?"

"Miss what?"

I explained, "Sorry, I meant to ask do you miss singing?"

"That's a hard question to answer. On one hand, I haven't really thought about it these past few years because I've had so much going on with GT and my clients. But when I was home pregnant with Ivy, I used to sing to her in my stomach all the time, and she would kick up a storm. After she died, I found myself singing just to feel closer to her. That's what I was doing when you and your brother came into the studio that day."

I grabbed her hand when I saw the tears gathering in her eyes. The last thing I wanted to do was make her sad when I promised to lift her spirits. I felt like Elle was getting out feelings, she had bottled up for way too long.

"You carry a piece of your angel everywhere you go, Elle. Ivy is your guardian angel and wants you to be happy and hold on to those memories of the two of you together. Even though she wasn't born yet, you two bonded and that's something that no one or circumstance can take away from you."

"Thank you, Savior, you don't know how much those words mean to me. It's been hard thinking about her without picturing me holding her lifeless body in the hospital. You made me remember the good times I had with her, and that's what I will hold on to."

Elle wiped the tears from her eyes with the hand I wasn't holding and smiled. I liked seeing her this way, with her eyes twinkling and happy. It was as if a weight was lifting off her as the day went on. Then an idea popped into my head to keep the smile on Elle's face, and to help her find the happiness she thought she'd lost. I just hoped, I wasn't pushing her too fast or she got the wrong idea.

"Elle, I want to take you somewhere, but I don't want you to think I have an ulterior motive."

"Shoot, where do you want to take me, and it bet not be to your hotel room!"

Laughing, I responded, "Naw, nothing like that, I promise. But I do want to take you to the studio, so we can write a song for Ivy. Something you can have with you always and listen to when you miss her."

Elle stared at me for a moment with indecision. I could tell that she was struggling on going, and I was happy to see Pepper and Saveon walk up at the same time. After telling them what my idea was, they both started trying to convince her to go.

"I don't want to get your hopes up, Savior and Saveon, on me singing on the album. If I record a song for my daughter, I know you will try to convince me to work with the both of you. You can't help it because music is your passion."

Nodding, I stated, "I'm not going to lie and say the thought didn't cross my mind. But this is really about you and Ivy, Elle. I also want you to rediscover your passion for singing. Because despite what you said, I see the sparkle in your eye when you talk about it. You said you want to find your happiness, why not see if one of your old loves will bring it back for you?"

"It can't hurt, plus, I would love to hear the voice that Savior and Saveon have been raving about." Pepper added.

We all nodded, then finally Elle responded, "Okay, let's go. If for nothing else but to have you all's help in putting together a song for Ivy. Plus, I can't lie and say the idea of actually singing in a studio doesn't bring up memories of me dreaming about it when I was younger. So, what the hell do I have to lose. I said, I was going to let go today and have fun while doing things that I want to do. Might as well live the dream and sing."

"Alright, then! Let me make a few calls, and we can head over to the studio I rented out for the month. I promise, you won't regret it."

We all got on the bus, and I watched Elle as we headed to the studio. Even though she was hesitant about going, there was a sparkle in her eye. No matter what I had to do, I was going to make sure that sparkle stayed there.

I watched as Matese sat on the edge of the small pool, staring out at nothing, smoking a blunt. He had been distant since Janiyah told him her news. I met her in the hospital waiting room a few months ago, and she told me that her name was Janiyah, but I didn't put two and two together. She was sitting there crying, and I talked to her until it was time for my lunch to end. Ever since then, she would pop up on whatever floor I was on to say hello and tell me how she was doing.

The whole situation was fucked up because how do you compete and fight for the man you love, against an ex he clearly still had feelings for and was dying? Janiyah was the mother of his first-born son, and I was the rebound. Despite what Matese said, I watched how he reacted to her from the window earlier. He was devastated that he was possibly losing the woman that he loved. I felt like shit for even feeling jealous when Janiyah was so sick, but I did. With her back and Maurice in the spare bedroom, was there even a place in Matese's life and heart for me and my baby?

As I turned to go out and check on him, I got nauseous as hell. This pregnancy was already taking me through it. Now the added stress of Janiyah coming back into our lives with Matese's son was just making it worse. I was trying to keep myself calm because the last thing I wanted to do was to lose my baby. But my nerves and heart were hurting, and I didn't know what to do to stop the pain.

"You want me to order some crackers and ginger ale from room service? It helped me when I was pregnant with Maurice and Yolanda," Janiyah asked.

"Um, no that's okay. Is Maurice asleep?"

She nodded and answered, "Yes, he's finally asleep. I was just about to head over to Mashelle's and give Yolanda a bath and head to bed. My back is killing me, and I'm exhausted."

"Janiyah, you need to make sure you are resting. Did Dr. Myers give you anything for the pain? Maybe I need to check your blood pressure because today has been a lot on everybody."

Janiyah replied, "He did give me something, but I left it back in Nashville. I left a message for Dr. Myers to call another prescription in, and I will pick it up in the morning."

"Okay, good. Have you decided on what you are going to do to fight it?"

She sighed and answered, "I have stage three ovarian cancer, Catrina. My odds aren't very good, and the last thing I want to do is spend the rest of the life I have left, throwing up and getting poison pushed into my veins."

"Don't look at it like that! There are so many treatments and clinical trials that can extend your life. You have two beautiful babies who need you, Janiyah, you need to fight for them."

Tears were now falling from her eyes, and I wrapped my arms around her and rubbed her back. My own tears fell with hers, at the enormity of her situation. It was one of the reasons I never wanted to go into Oncology because losing even one patient would kill me.

She finally pulled away and said, "Why are you still being so nice to me when you know who I am now?"

"Because no matter what the situation is, you needed a shoulder to cry on. What you are going through is heavy, Janiyah, and I would never mistreat you or your children just because we are both in love with the same man. It's just not in my nature. But like I said before, don't take my kindness as weakness. Matese is the one who has to make the decision on who and what he wants. Don't try to use your illness or any other underhanded tricks to get him back because karma is a bitch, and you have enough to deal with as it is."

We had a stare off, and she finally nodded her head and replied, "You don't have to worry about that. But I won't lie and say that I don't wish that Matese would choose me because I do. Matese was my first and only love. We were torn apart and never got the chance to finish our love story. He, the kids, and I are supposed to be a family and live out my last days together. When I came here, I never expected him to be here with a pregnant girlfriend. Especially, someone who I knew and has been there for me when no one else was. I feel bad because you don't deserve someone coming into your relationship and trying to tear it apart. It's fucked-up, Catrina, but I can't give up on him. I'm still in love with Matese, and I always will be."

"Here's the thing, Janiyah. Just because you were his first love, doesn't mean he can't feel anything for me, but that's not true. You might have been his first, but I'm the woman who stood by him and picked up the pieces when you broke his heart. The one who cheered him on and gave him all my love, support, and time to help him become the man he is now. We are in love and talking about a future together. I'm carrying his child, that he thanked God for when we got the results. Now, if by some reason he doesn't want to be with me anymore, then I will move on, and you can have the family you always wanted. But If he chooses me, then I expect you to do the same. As I said before, it's Matese's decision on who he wants to be with. We will just have to wait and see what his choice is, then deal with the consequences."

Janiyah said, "Fine. In the meantime, don't forget to have your friend come by and do the paternity test tomorrow. I want Matese to know for a fact that Maurice is his son."

"He will be here at ten tomorrow morning. If you don't mind, I told him to check on you too. You need a doctor here while we are in Vegas, if nothing else but to help manage your symptoms."

Frowning, she responded, "I appreciate that a lot. It isn't fair that I like the woman who could snatch away the one shot at happiness, besides my kids, that I have left. I never thought it would be this hard."

"Me either, believe me, I thought we were headed into our future together. But for the time being, we need to give Matese his space. I can help you with the kids if you need to rest, which you really should do. I'm hoping it will give you time to make the right decision regarding your treatment. If nothing else, instead of months, you could gain years with your babies. I can get with some colleagues of mine and see what they have out as far as trials as well. Just don't give up before you have weighed all your options."

She nodded and said, "I will think about it. The thing I hate the most, is that one of us is going to be destroyed once he makes his choice. You know it would be easier to let me die, Catrina, then you would have Matese all to yourself."

"Janiyah, if I have to wish death on someone to make a man choose to love me, I don't want or need that type of love. I'm going to head to bed, I promise to check on Maurice before I go to sleep."

Janiyah nodded and headed for the door. When she got to it, she turned around and said, "Thank you again, Catrina, for always being there when I needed you at the hospital. Whether you know it or not, you saved me in more ways than you will ever know, goodnight."

"Goodnight, Janiyah."

Janiyah left, and I was still standing there, mulling over our conversation. I watched her walk to Mashelle's villa and could tell she was in pain. Pulling out my phone, I sent a text to my friend and told him about her condition and to bring her something in the morning. Then I called the butler who was in charge of our villas and had him send someone with some Epsom salt and Aleve to hold her over for tonight. Then asked him to bring me some ginger ale and take Matese a bottle of

Crown. It was one of the only things that calmed him down. I was going down to him at first, but he needed his alone time.

I knew he was worried about Janiyah and having to choose between the two of us, but there was something else on his mind as well. Whatever it was, I hoped he figured it out because I didn't like to see him in pain. Matese was such a good man and deserved to be happy after everything he had been through.

Once I went into our bedroom, there was a red rose with a note that simply read, *"I love you, Trina."* Tears fell from my eyes, as I rubbed my stomach and thought about how much I loved Matese and all the good times we've had over the past year. We had finally gotten to a good place, and now, everything was turning to shit.

Janiyah was right about one thing, one of us was going to be left devastated once Matese made his choice. I just prayed it wasn't me and my baby.

AT THE STUDIO

"How do you like this line right here?"

I nodded as I read what Savior had written down. It amazed me how he was able to turn my feelings into music. The words flowed so effortlessly from his mind, and this song was everything I'd been feeling over the past few months.

"I love this part especially. My world was torn apart and being without her is unbearable. It's like you went inside of me and pulled out the words."

"Good, I'm glad you love it because I want this to be about you and Ivy. The song should showcase your connection and bond with her while you were pregnant and how losing her affected you, and how her memory helps get you through the day. I just need to work on some beats to put with this, so we can get everything down. Damn, is that the time?"

Looking at the clock, I saw it was eight at night. We had been brainstorming on Ivy's song for hours, and it was the first time in a long time, where I felt like this was home. Saveon and Pepper went to go and pick up food thirty minutes ago because we were in the zone.

"I haven't even been looking at the time. This has been so much fun, and I'm shocked by how much I don't want to leave right now. Let me check my phone because I know my mama is having a damn fit."

"It's because this is your passion, Elle. You know the next step is getting into the booth and trying out the microphone. I have tracks for just about any song you want to sing, since we still have a lot of work to do with the lyrics and music to Ivy's song. Come on, you've come this far, you might as well go all in."

Biting my lip, I looked over at the room I had dreamed of being in since I was little. Because Grant never wanted me to get anywhere near a booth, this had been the first time I'd been near one with the chance to actually sing. He wasn't here to tell me not to go in, and for the first time in months, my mind was screaming fuck Grant! He was selfish and only thought about his dreams, and I was stupid enough to give up mine, thinking I was standing by my man. "Alright, do you have Listen by Beyoncé?"

"I should have known you would pick something by Queen Bey. Yeah, I got you. Let me show you what to do, then you can do your thing. Follow me."

Savior opened the booth door and let me go in first. Standing there, I took every detail in as I looked around and touched the microphone and headset. Excitement coursed through my veins, and it felt like I was dreaming.

"It feels good, doesn't it? Like slipping into some warm water that soothes your soul."

Whipping around, I bumped into Savior, and we both stared at each other. With the two of us in here, it was tight, and his cologne filled the small room. I swallowed at his closeness and felt my body clench. There was no denying that he was fine as hell and being this close to him, made it more apparent. But more than his looks, there was a kindness and infectious spirit that added to the whole package that made up Savior Morrison.

Trying to break the tension between us, I asked, "Are you going to sing something too?"

A sad look crossed his face as he stepped back and answered, "Naw, I don't sing anymore. Writing is my thing now, and I love helping bring people's voices to the masses as they sing the songs I create. I used to sing to my wife, Lake, and the baby every night before we went to bed. Saveon even got me to sing a few times with him, but my heart's just not in it anymore. The singer in me died the same day they did. But enough about that, let's get you set up, so you can fall back in love with singing."

"I'm sorry, Savior."

He shook his head and responded, "Don't be, it's not your fault. Here, put on the headphones and just sing into the microphone. That's all there is to it."

Nodding, I watched as he stepped out of the booth and closed the door. Placing the headphones on and it got so quiet in the little room, I could hear my heart beating. Savior was now in front of me at the equipment and my palms started sweating. The enormity of what was about to happen hit me like a ton of bricks. I was about to sing for one of the biggest music producers in the world. This was something I dreamed about all my life, but what if I had waited too long and my voice was nothing special.

Savior must have seen my hesitation because the next thing I heard was his deep calm voice in my ears. "Get out of your head, Elle. Forget about GT, your pain, and all the noise in your head. Don't worry about who likes what and if you are hitting the right notes. What I want you to do is close your eyes, listen to the music, and just sing from your heart."

"Okay, I'll try to."

He shook his head and countered, "No, you are going to do exactly what I said and just sing. Now close your eyes, and I'm about to start the music."

I did as Savior said and closed my eyes, then cleared my mind of all the noise. There was nothing but silence. When the music started, it was automatic. My body was calm, and I felt the music fill my soul and my voice took over. All the years of Grant holding me back because of his selfishness came pouring out of me into "Listen".

By the time I sang the last note, tears were streaming from my eyes, and I was breathing heavily. I heard clapping in my ears, and my eyes instantly popped open. Savior, Pepper, and Saveon were standing up clapping. Pepper was even wiping away tears from her face.

"Come on out here, so you can listen to what we have been telling you from the beginning."

Taking off the headphones, I headed out of the booth into the control room. Pepper hugged me and said, "They were not exaggerating when they said you were an amazing singer. God blessed you with some serious pipes!"

"I don't know about all that. I just did what Savior said and sang from my heart."

Saveon stepped up and said, "My brother is a beast at bringing out the best in people's voices. But you have to have the talent to begin with."

"Yeah, just listen to how dope you are, Elle. I recorded it just so you could hear what Pepper, Saveon, and I heard."

Savior pushed a few buttons and my voice filled the air. My mouth hung open as I heard myself singing. I couldn't even believe it was me sounding like I was on the radio.

"I can't believe that's me. I can really sing."

"Hell yeah, you can sing! That's what I have been trying to tell you all along. If you want to, we could spend the rest of the night working on Ivy's song and record it. Pepper and Saveon brought us some dinner, so we could start after we finish eating. As a matter of fact, I want to let you in on a little secret. I'm announcing after the Star Awards that I am starting my own record label. Saveon is the first male artist I am signing, and I want you to be the first female I sign. That's how much I believe in your talent, Elle."

Before I could answer, my phone buzzed on the counter. I forgot to take it off silent from this morning. Looking at my screen, I saw I had over thirty missed calls and twenty text messages from Grant, Brooke, and my Mama.

"Hold on, let me let them know I'm okay."

"Alright, I'm going to work on some beats for Ivy's song."

Nodding, I stepped over to the side and dialed Grant's number.

"Where the fuck are you, Elle? I had plans for us tonight to go to a party and your simple ass went ghost on me!"

Frowning, I replied, "Why the hell are you yelling at me? I never promised to go to any party with you, Grant. As a matter of fact, I thought you weren't supposed to be getting into town until tomorrow?"

"Don't worry about when the fuck I got here! You need to meet me at Caesars Palace in an hour and wear something sexy!"

Shaking my head, I said, "I have plans, Grant."

"You got plans? Would those plans have anything to do with you hoeing your ass around Vegas with Savior Morrison? I mean, all the gossip sites have been talking about you and him sightseeing and shit through Vegas. I didn't take you for a dick chaser, but maybe I'm wrong. If you think he really wants to put you on his brother's album, then you are dumber than I thought. He only wants to fuck you, so he can get back at me. Watch, he is going to fuck you in every hole, then dumb your no talent ass off for me to pick up the pieces!"

At this point, I was fed the fuck up! I just wanted one fucking night to myself, and he just had to kill my fucking mood! Nope, enough was enough!

"Grant, you don't have to worry who I am fucking or singing for. I've put up with too much of your shit over the years, and I am fed up! We are done! I will ship you your gaudy ass ring, and you can mail me my shit, or you know what, just keep it! Fuck you and your fifty thousand skanks and your cum-sucking, hoe ass, diseased dick!"

I hung up before he could say another word. My blood pressure was through the roof, but I never felt so free in my life. The power I thought I had lost was coming back full force. The old Elle was gone, and I was ready to find the new me. The one who did what made her happy and didn't take shit from anyone.

"Elle, are you alright?" Savior questioned as Pepper and Saveon looked at me with concern.

I realized they had heard everything that went down between Grant and me. The concern was genuine in their faces, but I didn't need it. For the first time in a long time, I was living my life the way Elle wanted. Smiling to myself, I knew right then and there, it was time to take a big leap of faith.

Walking over to Savior, I reached out my hand and said, "Looks like you have yourself a new female artist."

"Girl, that mutherfucker had the nerve to show up at my house at two in the morning, trying to get in! I changed the locks on his ass since he called himself sleeping with his baby mama!"

I heard this loud ass woman yelling as I fought hard to open my eyes. My whole body felt heavy and there was pain throughout it. Finally, I pried my eyes open and realized I was in a hospital room.

The loud ass lady was in the hallway, outside my door. I wanted to yell and tell her to shut the hell up because my head was pounding, but I had a tube down my throat, preventing me from saying shit.

To the right of me, I saw my mama asleep in the chair beside my bed. Moving my hand, I pulled on her finger, trying to wake her up. Even moving that much hurt like hell. Finally, she moved and opened her eyes.

"Thank you, Jesus, my baby is awake! Hold on, Yo'Anthony.

Let me get the doctor, so they can get the tube out of your throat. You've been out of it, but I remembered what you told me in the ambulance when I found you. I had your brother move everything from the storage locker to my basement."

I nodded softly because my head was booming, but I was glad my mama had my back. While my Mama went to get the doctors, I laid there and thought about my bitch ass wife! Yes, I had married the hoe when she got pregnant with Yolanda.

Sad thing was is that I loved her, but she only had eyes for Matese. We all grew up together, and I always had the biggest crush on Janiyah. When we were in middle school, I was going to ask her to the dance, but Matese beat me to it. Just like he did when we were in the game. I was supposed to be the man, but of course, everyone flocked to Tese like he was the second coming or something. He had everything, and I had his leftovers.

So, when the time came for me to get rid of him, I took that shit and ran with it. Every day, I would follow Janiyah home from high school just to be close to her and record her taking her clothes off, so I could watch it later in my room.

This day was different. Some heavy shit went down, and I watched Matese commit his first murder. I followed him and got him on camera tossing the gun. Then grabbed it and hid it in a safe place to use when I needed it. I wanted to use it then, but it wasn't the right time.

Matese was doing well in the game, and I needed to know how he was doing it. Despite being his best friend, it took me years to get him to trust me enough to put me on. Once I was on the inside, I started gathering information until I knew every detail. Then I set him up and took everything from him that was supposed to be mine, including his woman and first born.

Now he was out, and Janiyah thought she could leave me and take my daughter with her! She didn't realize I knew exactly how to find her, or Janiyah would have made sure I was dead. I just needed to put some things in motion to make sure Matese wouldn't be a problem. Then, I was going to go and get my family back.

What Janiyah failed to realize is we were together til death do us part. I was going to show her and that little bastard exactly what that meant if they didn't fall in line.

"GT, you need to put that bitch on blast! I can't believe her hoe ass hasn't been here in three days! Did you ask her mama where she changed hotels to?"

Taking another sip of the Crown, I was drinking to calm my nerves down, as I thought about my break-up with my fiancée. She had blocked me and changed hotels. Elle breaking up with me wasn't new, but the way she was acting, was. Usually, I could talk her into meeting up with me, so we could talk shit out. Then, I would eat the fuck out of her pussy and put this dick in her life, and she would tighten up and come back to me. This time, it was silence, except for the numerous pictures on the blogs of her and Savior all over Vegas. She was making me look like a fucking sucker, and it was fucking with my ego like a mutherfucker!

"I called Elle's mama, and she doesn't know where she is

either because she's not responding to her too. I made sure to give her a little incentive to get the information for me though. So, she should have it soon since Elle doesn't go too long without talking to her mama."

Brooke stopped her pacing in front of me and said, "Why are you so fucking calm, GT! She fucked-up our plans with Big Tex! Now, the gossip blogs are having a field day with this love triangle shit! You need to let me blast her hoe ass and make her look like the money, fame-chasing hoe she is!"

"I'm thinking, Brooke, damn! Do you see I'm heartbroken because the woman I love dumped my ass over the phone? All you think about is how shit looks! What about my fucking feelings!"

She scoffed and countered, "You mean the same woman you were going to drug and let another man fuck? That woman you love. Stop the bullshit, GT, we both know the only reason you care, is because your little ego was stomped on. Well, you need to get off your ass and spin this story in your favor. You are out here looking weak as fuck as your fiancée runs around with your producer! Let me leak the story of you and Raven. We can say that you dumped Elle a few weeks ago and are here in Vegas with your new fiancée, the mother of your children."

The last thing I needed was Elle to find out I had not one, but two kids on her before I got her back. I know, I said we were through before but seeing her walking around happy with another man was doing something to me. Elle was mine, and I wanted her back, fuck the plan and Raven.

"Naw, sis. I changed my mind. Look, I know Elle, and she

wouldn't just hop into bed with Savior. My guess is he talked her into doing his brother's album, and she is doing it to get back at me. Do you still have connections with Jasper Brinks? I think, I can get Elle to come back to me if I can get Jasper to produce an album for her. I'll come off looking like the hero and once she has this singing shit out of her system, we can get married and everything will go back to normal."

"GT, have you lost your damn mind? Why do you keep trying to hold on to someone who doesn't want you or accept you for who you are? Elle ain't nobody, but Raven is! She's the mother of your kids and can make us a lot of money and new business opportunities! Fuck Elle's plain ass!"

Looking up at my sister, I asked, "What do you have against Elle, Brooke? I mean, you two used to be thick as fucking thieves, and now you act like you two were never best friends."

"I've outgrown her, bruh, and so have you. We always said that once we made it famous, we weren't going to let anyone or anything get in our way. Elle was supposed to be your backbone behind the scenes. But no, all she does is whine about who you are fucking and how you are never at home. Then running around looking like she belongs in the Sears 2020 catalog. I'm sorry, but money over friends for me."

I couldn't help but to shake my head at the bullshit my sister was spouting. I remember all the shit Brooke had been through over the years and my baby, Elle, had been there by her side no matter what. It had me looking at my sister sideways because her ass wasn't loyal to anything but money and fame.

"Damn, that's fucked up even for you, Brooke. You got me wondering if you will flip on me, and I'm your damn brother!"

"I will, if you try and go after Elle and fuck up the money, I have lined up for you and Raven! GT, I'm sorry, but you only want her ass back because you think Savior is fucking her. If you were really all that in love with her, you wouldn't be dropping babies in other bitches! Now, I have to go and handle some shit with the press, so you aren't out here looking like a fucking fool! Get your shit together, bro, and wash your ass and get dressed. Tonight, you will be hitting the club with Raven on your arm and acting like Elle doesn't even exist to you. I'm about to start leaking all kinds of dirt on Elle and make you look like a saint. Don't fuck up all my hard work because you are in your feelings. Remember, you are GT Wells and not nerdy ass Grant anymore."

"Whatever, Brooke! I know my baby, and she would never do me like that and fuck Savior! That pussy will always be mine, and Elle knows that!"

She laughed and responded, "Alright, GT, you keep telling yourself that! But I bet if I told you about the new sponsor for your upcoming tour with Raven, you would change your tune. BC Soda Company is putting close to fifty million dollars into your tour. All you have to do to capitalize on the deal is to stick with our plan and marry Raven. That's just the tip of the iceberg, GT. Think of the money we could make off your live wedding specials and wedding day photos. I might even be able to get you and Raven a reality show."

I downed the rest of my drink and poured another one. Brooke knew that money and fame was my weakness, which is why she knew that throwing both of them up would have me rethinking my plans to makeup with Elle. What people didn't know was that Elle was making almost as much money as I was now because she was in high demand for her choreography. I never thought she would get that much fame and money from dancing or I would have told her to sit her ass down somewhere. Brooke was right on one thing; I never wanted Elle to be in the spotlight. She was supposed to be my backup and stay in the shadows while I shined. In middle and high school, she was the star and I was the nerd, who they said was lucky to even have her as my girlfriend. I remember everyone acting like I was some charity case that Elle took on. Now it was my time to be the star, and she wouldn't let me shine. Why couldn't she just fall in line? "Fine Brooke, set the shit up, but if I talk to Elle, and she gets her shit together then it is what it is. As a matter of fact, just say that Raven and I are dating. Don't mention the engaged shit until I figure out what's going on with Elle."

"Bruh, I love you and all, but Savior is richer and finer than you. If Elle is smart, she will open up those legs and get on the Morrison gravy train. I hope she does because like I said before, y'alls relationship has run its course."

Before I could cuss my sister out, there was a knock on the door. Brooke walked over to open it as I downed my drink and poured another one. Pulling out my phone, I saw that Elle hadn't responded to my calls or texts. The shit was pissing me off even more.

"Brooke, I thought you had this shit under control! I did my part and fucked that walking dickslinger like you asked me to because you said you had a plan to get rid of Elle. But all I see is Elle living it up in Vegas with my man!" Kiara screamed as she stomped into the room.

I don't know why she was tripping because she had fucked other people for less. She was just good at hiding her shit. Shaking my head, I sat back and nursed my drink while my sister handled Kiara's whining ass.

"Kiara, fucking Big Tex isn't a chore. I can attest to riding that dick and it's always good, so you can stop fronting. As far as Elle goes, I'm handling it. Our original plan is a bust, but that doesn't mean I'm not thinking of other ways to get rid of her ass. You need to be worried about your pregnancy!"

My head whipped around as I slurred, "Damn, who nutted in your funky ass pussy! You probably don't know who the daddy is since you fuck a whole gang of men daily."

"Fuck you, GT! You are just pissed off I'm not fucking you anymore! Anyway, Brooke, I am trying to figure out how to get him to fuck me a few times, so I can make the pregnancy a reality. Savior might be mad, but he always has been weak for my pussy. I just need to get him alone, and I can let nature take its course."

Brooke and I both laughed because we knew Savior wasn't going to just fuck her after she leaked that damn video of his dick. He stayed cussing her ass out whenever they were near each other.

Brooke replied, "Now, Kiara, we all know Savior isn't messing with your ass anymore. You did that man dirty, and he gives not one fuck about you or your pussy."

"Alright, fine! But you don't have to laugh about it, Brooke! I came to you because Tex said you had some type of drugged bottle that you were going to use on Elle. Well, I want to use it on Savior, so I can make him relaxed enough and we can make a baby together."

This hoe was desperate, and I was glad I had let her crazy ass go earlier on in my career. I could tell even back then that she was a few cells short of looney.

"Yeah, it and it's already chocked full of Ecstasy, GHB, and a few others that I got from south of the border. There are enough aphrodisiacs in that bottle to make a nun turn into a hoe. But I had to pay a pretty penny for that bottle, so what makes you think I would just hand it over to you?"

Kiara scowled and responded, "Bitch, you told me I needed to get Savior back in order for me to get more jobs and fans! If I make more money, so do you!"

"Yeah, but I want more. That little fifteen percent doesn't include me doing illegal shit for you. That extra treatment is reserved for my VIP clients who pay me thirty percent."

Kiara was heated, and I couldn't help but laugh at my greedy ass sister. Brooke had Kiara right where she wanted her.

"Fine, Brooke, you can have thirty percent! But I expect you to get me more jobs and help me get Savior back! Whenever I need you, I expect you to be there no questions asked!"

My sister rolled her eyes, then responded, "I don't do threats, sweetheart, so you can cut out all that drama. Now follow me to my room, and I will get you the bottle. You do know it takes people years to get pregnant, right?"

"I've already been to a fertility doctor out here, and I'm ovulating. All I have to do is get some shit in his system and fuck him all night long. If that doesn't work, I have a sterile cup to collect his sperm and have myself inseminated. Tonight, there is a big party at the MGM Grand, and Savior is hosting it. His usual driver had to go back to Nashville for a family emergency, so I made sure to get in good with the new driver, and he is going to put the bottle in the car. I know Savior, and he always drinks Hennessey in the car ride over to parties. I've reserved the villa across from him, so I will wait for him to get back, so I can fuck him all night long."

I stared at her disturbed ass and said, "That's some sick and desperate shit, even for you, Kiara! I'm about to head to my room and take a nap. You bitches are scandalous!"

"GT, you were about to do worse, by drugging your fiancée and having another man fuck her on camera! Which one is worse? At least, I am going to be the one fucking my own man! Brooke, let's go because I need your help to make sure everything goes according to plan. Then, we need to come up with something to get rid of Elle. As a matter of fact, I bet he will have that bitch at the party tonight with him. Brooke, you need to get me a pass into the party."

"Yesssssssss, bitch! Now you are talking! As a matter of fact, I think we all need to go to the party and fuck some shit up! You know there will be plenty of paparazzi there just begging for a story, and we are going to give them what they want! Let me get ahold of Raven, so she can come through with us."

Shaking my head, I went into the bedroom of my suite and slammed the door. My buzz was officially killed when she put me in the same category as her and Brooke. Despite what I had been planning, I had never gone through with it and that had to account for something.

I flopped on the bed and closed my eyes. Visions of Elle

naked, riding my dick popped into my mind. Reaching in my pants, I pulled out my dick and started stroking it as I pictured Elle's titties bouncing, as she rode me hard and fast. My shit instantly went limp as the image changed, and she was orgasming on Savior's dick.

Growling, I hopped up and strode back to the living room in the suite and yelled, "I'm coming too! I need to talk to Elle and get her the fuck away from that mutherfucker!"

"Alright, GT, but don't be pissed off when you find out you put the wrong bitch on a pedestal. And ewww, next time put your dick up before you stroll your ass out here, making demands! I'm your sister and don't want to see your shit swinging! What the fuck was you doing in there any damn way?"

Stroking my shit, I replied, "Fuck you, Brooke! I'm trying to relieve some damn stress since I have been dealing with your ass all damn day! Get the fuck out if you don't want to see it, this is my gotdamn suite!"

"Kiara, please go and suck or ride his dick, so he can shut the fuck up! I got shit, I need to handle before tonight, so I got to go! Don't act offended either because we both know you used to ride that shit daily," Brooke demanded.

I was about to tell them to both kiss my ass. Kiara shrugged her shoulders, came over, and dropped to her knees, sucking the head of my dick in her mouth. My toes curled as I hung onto the doorframe as Kiara reminded me of why I used to think about wifing her over Elle.

Brooke left, and I spent the rest of the afternoon fucking Kiara. She was knocked out in the bed, while I surfed the blogs and got angrier as picture after picture of Savior and Elle popped up. The way he was looking at Elle made me think he was feeling her, but my baby would never cheat on me. She might be salty right now, but she knew that pussy belonged to me as well as her heart.

If Elle thought I was going to let her go, she and that mutherfucker had another thing coming!

"Remember to watch yourself tonight, Savior. The blogs are already having a field day with Kiara's pregnancy and you running around with GT Well's fiancée. I swear, you like making my job hard as hell!" Pepper stated.

I was standing in front of the mirror, eyeing the Gucci outfit the stylist had sent over for me to wear for this party. The jeans, black shirt, belt, and shoes matched to perfection. I had a few chains on and my Rolex. My barber had come and got my head and face straight earlier, so I was good to go.

"Pepper, you don't have to worry about me acting a fool because I know what's at stake. And stop saying that Kiara is pregnant because we all know that's a damn lie! Elle is my artist, and nothing is going on between us but music, friendship, and mutual respect."

Pepper eyed me, shook her head, and said, "It doesn't matter if she is pregnant or not, Savior, because the world believes it! As far as Elle goes, I'm happy you did listen to me and decided to announce your new label tonight at the party. Once you introduce Saveon and Elle as your first artists, then it will make sense on why you and she have been hanging out so much."

"Yeah, I gotta admit that announcing at the party was a good move. I'm trying to talk Elle into having her first live performance with Saveon onstage at the Star Awards. I want it to be a surprise to everyone. Did you contact the press and tell them to be at the party?"

She nodded and answered, "Yeah, I have all of them coming and then some. The stylist and makeup team are in Elle's room, making sure she is good for the big reveal. She looks gorgeous, Save. I am so happy you talked her into signing with you because Elle deserves some happiness in her life. Now, Saveon and I are leaving in about five minutes, because I have to be there early to make sure everything is the way you want it to be. Matese is going to be up here in a minute to escort you and Elle to your car, which should be arriving in fifteen minutes."

"Alright, that sounds like a plan. See you all at the party."

After Pepper left out, I heard a knock on the door before Matese's voice boomed through the suite. "You about ready, bruh?"

"Yeah, I'm ready. I'm surprised you are even coming, tonight, Tese. I would understand if you wanted to sit this one out, with everything you are going through."

Tese rubbed his head and replied, "Naw, I needed to work to keep my mind off all the drama in my life. Janiyah hasn't been feeling well, and Catrina is barely talking. Ever since the results came back that Maurice is mine; I've been trying to make up for lost time with my son. I still can't believe the situation I'm in."

Matese had been through it these past few days. To find out you have a five-year-old son, your first love is dying, and your current love is threatening to leave you, was a mutherfucker. I didn't know who he was going to choose, and the only thing I could do was be there for him.

"Damn, Tese. I'm sorry you are going through this shit, man. What are you going to do about Janiyah and Yo? Did Blast find anything in the storage locker?"

"Naw, by the time they got there, everything in that mutherfucker had been cleaned out. Yo was at General Hospital but he's been transferred, and no one knows to where. I don't like having an enemy lurking, I can't find. As far as Janiyah and Catrina goes, I don't know, man and it's fucking with me hard. Catrina is the woman who was there for me when I was starting over and is carrying my child. The ring has been burning a hole in my pocket since I picked it up. But now I'm afraid to ask her because she might say no. Hell, I wouldn't blame her with all the baggage I'm bringing with me."

"How are you feeling about Janiyah?"

He shook his head and responded, "I mean, I can't lie and say I don't have love for her because I do. Janiyah was my first everything and is the mother of my son. Despite all the pain she caused me, it hurts like hell to hear her say she is dying. Not to mention, she had to be with Yo to keep a needle out of my arm. How do I repay her for that shit?"

"You say you love her, and I get it, Tese. But are you in love with Janiyah?"

Tese sighed and answered, "I don't know, Save. How the fuck can I be in love with two women? In some ways, I wish Janiyah had stayed away and everything in my life would be perfect. But then, I wouldn't know about Maurice, and my son would still be getting abused by Yo."

"I wish, I had the answers to help you out, but you definitely need to figure out who you want to be with. You have two women who are in love with you and both of them of hurting because of it. I just don't want you to lose both of them in the process. Have you talked to your sister yet?"

"Naw, I am tomorrow before we head over to the Star Awards rehearsal. Jace is finally back, and I want her to enjoy the evening with him. But enough about my fucked-up love life, you know everyone's talking about you and Elle. I've got to ask if there is some truth to the rumors."

I laughed and said, "Not you, too! We are just friends and co-workers. She just got out of shit with her fiancé, and I'm not trying to be the rebound. Plus, Kiara's ass is lurking again, and I don't need her fucking with Elle."

"For someone who says they are just a friend, it seems like you at least gave it some thought. I mean, Elle is gorgeous and has that nice dancer's body. No one would blame you for shooting your shot."

I eyed him and responded, "Don't you have enough shit going on with women, Tese? You shouldn't be looking at her body."

"I'm a man, of course I looked! But seriously, Save, she seems like a good woman and you two seem to vibe really well."

Standing up, I checked myself one last time before heading

for the door. I didn't want to answer Matese because truth be told, these past few days had been some of the happiest I'd had in a long time. Elle was sweet, funny, and talented. It amazed me how she picked up on my moods and nuances as we worked together on lyrics and music. We just vibed like we had known each other for years. I didn't want to mess that up by complicating it with a romance that might not work out. Hell, look at how my relationship with Kiara turned out.

"Come on, Tese, we are going to be late. We need to pick up Elle from her suite and head over to the red carpet for the party. I want to get Elle seated and comfortable before the crowd gets there. This is her coming out as an artist, and I want her to be as relaxed as possible."

Matese laughed and said, "Yeah, alright, your silence is enough of an answer to me. Let's go and pick up your 'friend'."

Ignoring him, I allowed him to open the door and head out in front of me. When he first started as my bodyguard, it bothered me that he put himself in front of danger for me. But after a ton of arguing with Pepper, I finally gave in and let him do his job. Despite leaving my old life behind me, I was licensed to carry, so I stayed with a nine on me at all times.

We stopped in front of Elle's suite just as the makeup and hair people were leaving out. My stylist, Miyanda, was in the living room of the suite, putting clothes into bags as we walked in and closed the door.

"What's up Miyanda, did you get Elle straight?"

"Hey, Savior! I see you are looking good as ever in Gucci from head to toe!"

I laughed because I knew she was just playing with me. She

was very much still in love with my boy, but she would never admit that shit. Walking over, I rubbed her big belly and stated, "Yeah, you better quit flirting before Doom comes in and hears that shit! I don't feel like fighting tonight."

Miyanda rolled her eyes and retorted, "Fuck Doom, you know damn well we aren't together anymore. He fucked up any chance of us being together when he cheated on me with Brooke's evil ass! The only thing he can do for me is to help me take care of our daughter, who should be here in two months. Plus, that gorgeous woman in there will have all of your attention tonight. I'm heading over there now; do you have me on the list?"

"Yeah, but make sure you sit your ass down and don't go into labor at my shit, Miyanda. I don't know why you want to go anyway when you are so far along. You can have one of your assistants help keep Elle tight."

Shaking her head, she responded, "Nope, I'm tired of sitting at home by myself. Plus, Doom has a bodyguard following me around every damn where, so I will be just fine. I want to hang with Mashelle and Pepper tonight too, since I haven't seen them in ages. I hear your girl Catrina will be there too, right Matese?"

"Yeah, she's pregnant too, so both your asses need to make sure you are on that damn couch and nowhere else. I have a few of my guys as well guarding the VIP to make sure y'all are taken care of. They know to take you two down the back elevators if something pops off. So, don't be surprised if they drag y'all hard-headed asses out either," Matese ordered.

"Whatever, Matese. Make sure not to give Elle this bag I

picked out for her to wear with her outfit. See you all at the party!"

Miyanda left after we said goodbye. I made sure to hit Doom up and tell him Miyanda was going to be at the party tonight. She might not like it, but I owed him a head's up because he was the father of her child and needed to know where she was in case some shit popped off.

"Damn!" Matese growled.

"What the hell did you say that for?" I questioned, but soon saw why as I looked up from my phone.

Elle was standing in the doorway with a black Gucci dress with cutouts over her breasts that led to a V that ended with a triangle cutout, exposing her stomach. It had sheer long black sleeves, and the dress curved her slim toned hips and then flared out a bit. The dress had a slit that went up to her upper thigh and played peekaboo as she moved. Her toned chocolate legs were glowing and looked sexy as hell with her Gucci shoes to match.

Her natural hair had big ringlets in it, and I loved how the mass framed her face. Elle's makeup was on point, highlighting her features but not overpowering them. The dark lipstick on her lips had me wondering how those lips would feel on mine.

"Do you like it or is it too much? I told them I didn't want to straighten my hair, so we compromised with curls. Pepper said I had to dress up my look since I would be in the spotlight now. I'm just glad I still look like myself."

I wanted to reply, but my eyes were still taking every inch of Elle in.

"You look good, Elle! I think everyone is going to love your new look. I mean, you were gorgeous already, but now you look like a star," Matese stated.

Her face broke into a smile, then she looked over at me for my approval. Finally getting myself together I added, "Yeah, Miyanda and Pepper did the damn thing with your look. I can't wait to show you off to the world tonight. They need to see what I saw in you, the first time I saw you sing in the booth. A woman who was meant to be a star. You are stunning, Elle."

"Thank you, Savior, for the first time in a long time, I feel like one. Wow, I just realized that Miyanda matched us up! People are really going to be talking about us being a couple now."

Smiling, I replied, "They were talking anyway, so don't even worry about what they are going to say. Shit, we look good, and that's all that matters. Are you ready to go and tell the world you are ready to live your dream?"

"I'm nervous but ready to start living my life. If you have enough faith in me to sign me as an artist, then I have faith in you to help me launch my singing career. Just make sure there are plenty of drinks on hand to help with my nerves."

Grabbing her hand, I stated, "I've got drinks in the car as well as the VIP area, but you don't have to worry about being nervous. I will be with you every step of the way. Whenever you get nervous, just squeeze my hand, and I've got you."

Elle smiled, and we all headed downstairs and got in the limo that was waiting for us. As usual, Matese sat up front after he made sure Elle and I were in the back safely.

Once we settled in and pulled off, I noticed a bottle of

Hennessey with a bow on it. Knowing Pepper, she probably left it for me, so I could pregame before we got to the party.

"Hey, you want a drink before we hit the red carpet?" I asked.

"No, brown liquor isn't my thing, but can I have some of the champagne over there?"

Smiling, I put the bottle of Hennessey down and popped the champagne. After pouring us both a glass, I handed her one then raised mine and said, "Here's to the start of my record label, your singing career, and successful partnership in music."

"Here, here!"

We clinked glasses and took sips as we enjoyed the ride. I couldn't help but to appreciate the view of legs that Elle was showcasing as her dress rode up. She was so fucking fine; it was messing with my resolve to keep it strictly business between us.

Soon, we pulled up to the MGM, and I helped Elle out. Lights were flashing everywhere, capturing every move we made. I placed my hand on her back as we followed Matese and Vern, my other bodyguard, followed behind us. The last thing I wanted was for Elle to get caught up in these crowds, without protection.

Leaning down, I whispered, "Are you alright?"

"Yes, I'm used to walking the carpets with GT, but no one really paid me any attention. This time, I feel like I'm on display."

Pulling her closer into me, I nodded and kept her wrapped in my arms until we got to the area to take pictures.

"Savior, what about Kiara's pregnancy? Are you going to be a deadbeat dad? Elle, is it true you left GT because Savior makes more money! Over here! We need a picture of the new it couple! Awwwwwww, you all are matching!" paparazzi yelled out at us.

Before I could go off, Pepper came from out of nowhere and said to the rowdy crowd, "Okay, Savior and Elle are available for just a few pictures, and then they have to head inside. You don't want to miss the announcement, so please don't keep them long. Thank you!"

"Elle, we don't have to do this shit. We can head inside and say fuck these vultures!"

She shook her head and replied, "No, we might as well get this over with. Plus, this is going to be my life soon. So, I might as well accept the bad with the good and get used to it."

"Alright, but only a few pics then we will head in and get a few drinks before the announcements."

She nodded, then we posed for a few pictures. When we were finished, Pepper ushered us into the elevator, leading to our VIP section. As soon as the doors opened, we were greeted by the music bumping in the party. Our section had its own bar, dance floor, and bathrooms. Tonight, I didn't want to have to deal with autographs or mutherfuckers bothering us. I wanted to celebrate my new label and artists in peace.

We sat down on the huge white sectional and ordered our drinks. Saveon, Pepper, Matese, Catrina, Mashelle, Doom, Jace, and Miyanda were all around us, already sipping and talking.

.   .   .

Elle turned to the women and started talking while I slapped hands with my boys, Jace, Doom, and Saveon. Matese joined us as we caught up with each other.

"What's up, Jace, I haven't seen you in a minute?" I asked.

"Man, just been trying to maintain. Business is booming, and I'm just trying to keep up with the demand. Not to mention, trying to spend as much time with my babies. My son, Zen, is bad as hell, man, and my princess, Diamond, is hitting the hell out of my pockets. But other than that, just trying to keep my woman and family happy."

Jace used to be a doctor, but had his license revoked due to some shit that wasn't his fault. Now, he ran a lucrative prescription drug ring, along with an underground organ ring with his sister, Kut. He was also dating Tese's sister, Mashelle.

"Yeah, I feel you. I was hoping Alexis and Kevell would be able to come tonight, but they won't be able to be here until next week," Matese added.

I smiled because Alexis was a trip. She loved flirting with me to get a rise out of her husband, Kevell, who was one my best friends from back in the day. He, Saveon, and I used to run the streets together. Kevell used to run drugs while Saveon and I ran a high-end stolen car ring. We all went legit around the same time.

"That's what's up! I can't wait to see my baby mama, Alexis."

"Yeah, alright, with that baby mama shit! Don't let my sister get you fucked up! You know Kevell don't play about his wife!" Jace joked.

We all laughed, and I saw that Doom wasn't paying us any

attention. He was too busy staring Miyanda down as she chatted with Elle. Matese, Saveon, and Jace went to go over to the hookah area, where Mashelle and Pepper were. It gave me a chance to holler at Doom one-on-one.

"Why don't you just tell Miyanda you love her and get on your knees and beg for forgiveness?" I asked.

"I wish it was that simple, Save, but Miyanda was done with me as soon as I cheated on her with Brooke. It didn't help that Brooke and I were in a whole relationship after she left me either. Man, I should have listened when you told me not to mess with that hoe! She cost me the love of my life."

Shaking my head, I couldn't say shit because I told him not to fuck up his relationship with Miyanda. But he was hard-headed and let his dick mess up his happy home.

"I'm sorry, Doom, just give her some time. You all are about to have a beautiful baby girl and hopefully, that will bring you two back together. But on the real, don't fuck with her if you aren't ready to give up the extra pussy you are used to getting. Miyanda doesn't deserve that, Doom."

"Yeah, I hear you, man, which is why I haven't tried to get back with her. I still have a lot of growing up to do. I just hope no one steals her away from me, before then. Speaking of women, when are you going to get one? Or do you already have someone in mind?" he responded, nodding towards Elle.

Elle was rubbing Miyanda's stomach and laughing at something Catrina said. Her skin was glowing, and she was looking sexy as hell with her thigh exposed. I had to adjust myself because my mind was going to a dangerous place.

"She is fine as fuck, but you know how I feel about messing

with artists. We are just beginning our business relationship and friendship. I don't want to mess up what we have going on right now."

"Shit, fuck that, Save. You have to find happiness wherever you can. Don't think I didn't pick up on you touching her every chance you get. Are you sure you aren't going there because of Lake?"

It took me a minute to answer because I never thought about it like that. With Kiara, I knew it wasn't going anywhere, so I wasn't thinking about forever with her. After getting to know Elle, I knew she was the type of woman who wanted it all. The marriage, picket fence, and a basketball team of kids. Having my wife and child murdered in front of me, had me terrified of that shit happening again. There was no way in hell, my heart could take another loss like that.

"Not going to lie and say that Lake isn't a big part of me not having a serious relationship because her death has a lot to do with it. Do you know how it feels to know my own cousin murdered my wife on some jealous shit? I would have gladly given him the whole car theft ring in order to have my wife and child here with me today. Yeah, I'm not dirty anymore, but Elle is the type of woman you wife. I don't want to give my heart to another woman just to have her snatched away."

"Save, you can't think that way. Hell, any of us could die at any time because we all have an expiration date. But what you need to realize is, life is too short to live with regrets. You've always been a man who wanted a wife and kids. When you talk about Pepper and Saveon, I hear how much you want that for yourself. You were fearless when you dove headfirst into this industry and look at all the shit you have accomplished. Don't shortchange yourself personally because you're scared. I'm about to head over with Saveon and them because you got me over here getting all philosophical and shit. Just think about what I said. You coming over?"

"Naw, it's almost time for the announcement, so I'm just going to chill here for a minute. But I heard you, Doom. Don't forget what I said too. Just because you fucked up, doesn't mean you can't change."

Doom nodded and headed over to the hookah area. I sat back and down the rest of my Hennessey. It felt good to have all my people here ready to turn up and celebrate this new chapter in my life. After talking to Doom about my love life, it made me wish that Lake was here to share this moment with me.

"Hey, you got this sad look on your face. Are you alright?" Elle questioned as she sat down beside me.

"Yeah, just had a moment you know. I look around and think about everything I've accomplished and wish Lake was still here with me. She should have been here by my side as I announced the start of Morrison Records."

Elle grabbed my hand and commented, "But she is here, Savior. Lake is here watching you shine and excel in your life, despite the pain of losing her and your child. You are a survivor, Savior, and you should celebrate that tonight for them."

"Thanks, Elle. I know you are right. I'm going to honor Lake and my child tonight, by celebrating. Lake's birthday is next week, and usually, I am living in the studio or in a hotel with a case of Hennessey. But you've kept my mind off it by keeping my mind occupied, and I'm grateful, Elle."

I watched her blush as I squeezed her hand back and got lost in her chocolate-colored eyes. Those plump lips of hers was begging to be kissed and sucked on. The pull between us was strong, and it was as if a magnet was pulling us toward each other. Just as I was about to give into temptation, Pepper walked up.

"Sorry to interrupt you two, but it's time for the announcement. The press is in their spot below, and the DJ is ready whenever you are and has the snippets to Saveon's album and Elle's first song," Pepper interrupted.

"Do you think the first song is good enough, Savior? I mean, we haven't finished it yet, and the voice coach is still working to help me improve."

"Naw, it's perfect just the way it is. It's just enough to showcase your voice and leave them wanting more. We are going to do Saveon's music first, so we can get the crowd hype, then show them the real Elle Jamison. Come on superstar, and remember I gotcha, so don't be nervous."

"I'll try not to."

Once we made it to the stage, my brother and I stepped forward as Pepper stood at Saveon's side and Elle stood at mine.

"What's up everyone? I know you all are ready to party and drink up all my alcohol, so I won't be long. Tonight, I'm pleased to announce something me and my brother used to dream about when we were younger. We always had a passion for music and said that one day, we would team up and become a powerhouse in this industry. Well, I am pleased to announce, the beginning of our dream with the start of our own label, Morrison Records!"

The crowd went wild as cameras flashed at the news. Saveon then announced his crossover into R&B and becoming my first male artist on the label. My brother liked to say it was just my record company, but as soon as he was ready to step back from the limelight, it would be ours. I knew my parents, sister, Faith, Lake, and my child, were all looking down on us and smiling.

My brother was finishing up his speech, so I turned to Elle and whispered, "Are you ready?"

"As ready as I will ever be. But I don't want to give a speech, not right now at least."

"I gotcha, gorgeous. Just let me make the announcement, then we can go and just chill in VIP for the rest of the night."

Elle smiled, and I felt a twinge in my chest. It just felt right having her by my side and that still scared me.

Turning around, Saveon handed me the microphone, and I grabbed Elle's hand and pulled her forward.

"Alright, everyone. I'd like to introduce you to a beautiful lady that you all know for her talents as one of the hottest chore-ographers in the industry. But what you don't know is that she can also sing her ass off! That's why when I heard her sing, I knew we had to sign Elle Jamison as our first female artist on Morrison Records! Now, the DJ is about to give you all a peek of what's to come from Saveon and Elle, our debut artists at Morrison Records. I want everyone to grab some drinks, eat this expensive ass food, and listen to some dope ass music! DJ Spin, drop that shit!"

"You heard the man of the hour, the hottest producer in the biz, and now owner of Morrison Records! Are you ready Vegas to hear what Saveon and Elle are about to hit you with!" DJ Spin yelled.

"YESSSSSSSSSSSS!" the crowd screamed.

Saveon's song boomed through the speakers and everyone started dancing and swaying to my brother's new R&B sound.

Elle's hand was squeezing the shit out of my hand as pictures and questions started pouring from the press in front of us. Her palms were moist, and I could feel the tremble in her body. I needed to get her away from here, so I could calm her down. Luckily, Pepper answered most of the questions for us. Then told them that she would be sending out a press statement.

Guiding Elle through the crowd of well wishers and nosey ass people, I headed straight to the elevator. Once the doors closed, I pulled Elle into my arms and held her, hoping she wasn't regretting signing with me. The thought of stage fright never popped in my mind because she was used to dancing on stage in front of millions of people.

I rubbed my hand through her curls and inhaled the fruity scent of her hair. Elle's body curved to mine perfectly, and my dick twitched as she snuggled into my chest. But she didn't need that right now.

"Elle, if you changed your mind, I understand. Singing in front of people isn't easy, I'm sorry if I pushed you too fast."

She pulled away from me with a smile on her face, and explained, "No, it's not stage fright. It just hit me up there that something that I've wanted for so long, has finally happened for me. All these emotions went through me, standing there and hearing my name and female artist in the same sentence. It was everything I dreamed of and even more, Savior. Is it bad that I don't want to stay for the party and go to the studio instead? I just want to sing and pour all of these emotions into my music."

"Damn, you had me worried there for a minute, Elle. But you sound like me the first time I heard one of my songs on the radio. There's nothing like that feeling of knowing you are about to have the one thing you have always wanted. We don't have to stay for the whole party, but we do need to at least be here at least an hour to hear the samples being played. Then, I promise we can work as long as you want in the studio tonight."

She smiled and replied, "That sounds like a deal to me. I could use a few drinks to loosen up."

"Alright then, let's grab some drinks and hang with our people, then we will head out."

"Thank you again, Savior, for believing in me. You have no idea how you have helped me through a difficult time. Not to mention, making my dreams come true."

She leaned over and kissed me on the cheek. My first instinct was to pull her in and kiss her, but the doors to the elevator opened up and a crowd was standing there clapping.

I wrapped my arm around Elle's waist and pulled her closer into my side. We made our way to our section of the VIP area, while thanking fans and colleagues. I made sure to introduce Elle to some of the more important players of the industry. All though Elle was nervous and new to this, she did well with meeting and captivating them. I wasn't surprised because she had a good vibe about her. Everyone was excited about Morrison Records and was looking forward to what we had coming.

Everything was going good, and I couldn't wait to get to VIP and celebrate, then hit up the studio. There was this song in my head, and I wanted to get it on paper. We had been mingling for the past thirty minutes, and it was almost time for Elle's snippet to play. I wanted to be with our people, so she could enjoy this moment in peace.

"You did good and everyone loves you. Are you ready to get something to drink now?" I stated, whispering in Elle's ear.

She smiled and grabbed my neck, pulled me down, and whispered, "Yes, because my feet are killing me in these heels. Plus, it's getting hot in here, I'm sure I look a mess now."

Pushing a curl away from her eye, I rubbed her face and said, "Naw, never that. You look beautiful, Elle. Don't let anybody tell you differently."

"Savior, why are you hugged up on this bitch while I am at home alone, carrying your baby!" Kiara screamed as she stormed towards us with her entourage, recording everything.

"Elle, head over to Pepper and Saveon. Your song is about to play, I want you to watch the reactions of the crowd once they hear your voice. I don't want you in the middle of this mess, with Kiara."

She asked, "Are you sure you don't need backup?"

"I got this, you just go and celebrate because we have a long night ahead of us in the studio."

Elle nodded, and headed on to our VIP area. I turned to Kiara and said, "You have five minutes to get the fuck out of my party, before I have you thrown out! I'm tired of your shit, and you need to stay far away from me before I do something, we both regret!"

"Did you all hear him threaten me? Jackie, did you get that on live? I want the whole world to see how the father of my child and the man that I love treats me! Savior, I can't believe you left me for Elle Jamison! How many times have I asked you to write me a song or help me with my singing career? How long did it take that bitch on her knees, to earn a spot on your record label?"

I waved Vern over, so he could take this ditzy bitch and her dick hungry hoes with her. This stalking shit was getting out of hand. If she wanted to put on a show for the world, I was about to give them one to remember.

"For one, if you are pregnant, we both know that baby ain't mine. Even when we were going heavy, I wrapped my shit up twice! Secondly, Elle and I are just friends, something you know nothing about since your so-called friends stay in my DM's begging for me to fuck them. Finally, Kiara, you can't sing! The only tune you can carry is when you are humming on some dick! Now, for the last fucking time, stop stalking me because you and I are over! Vern, get their asses out of here and make sure they don't come back!"

"I gotcha, Mr. Morrison! Tony, grab them, so we can get them out of here. Let's go, ladies!"

"Let go of me, I'm pregnant! Savior, you are going to pay for fucking me over! You and that bitch!" Kiara screamed as she and her minions cussed and made a fucking scene as usual. Now, my party had turned into a fucking ratchet reality show!

Pepper ran over to me and I held up a hand to stop her and said, "I already know what you are going to say, Pepper. Vern just escorted them out, and I'm going to talk to my attorney about the restraining order."

"That's good, but that's not why I am here. Your brother is about to beat Elle's ex-fiancé's ass! You need to get over there now because GT is about to make Saveon lose his religion."

Looking over at VIP, I saw Saveon and GT standing toe to toe with each other. Brooke and Raven were also there. They were arguing with Elle and Miyanda. I knew my party was about to turn into World War Ten. So much for celebrating. I had a feeling the night was about to end with me knocking a mutherfucker out.

"HEY, BOO! CONGRATULATIONS ON YOUR RECORD DEAL!" Mashelle yelled as I walked into Savior's section.

The past few days, I'd hung out with Mashelle, Catrina, and Pepper. It had been a long time since I had any new female friends. My so-called best friend, Brooke, had soured me from having them because of how wishy washy she had become. Miyanda was someone I had met today, but we instantly clicked, and I loved her personality.

Doom and Jace were in the hookah area, while Saveon and Pepper were still mingling with the crowd. I looked over at Savior, and he and Kiara were still arguing.

"Thank you, Shelle! I was soooooooo nervous!"

"Girl, you couldn't tell at all! You know you and Savior look like a power couple up there together. All black love goals and shit!" Mashelle commented.

I blushed because it was flattering, but we were just friends. "No, Savior has a lot of drama going on with Kiara right now, and I just broke off my engagement. We work well together in the studio, and that's as far as that will go."

"Girl, he is not thinking about Kiara, that girl showed the world that man's dick without permission. She only wants to use him for his name. I'll be back, this baby has me running to the bathroom every five minutes," Catrina added.

"I'll go with you, Trina, since Matese is working. I don't want any of these assholes to bump into my niece or nephew," Mashelle stated as they got up and left.

Miyanda was rubbing her back, and I frowned. "Are you okay?"

"Girl yes, my back is killing me! After your song, I'm going to head back to the hotel and soak in the jetted tub in my villa, with a tub of chocolate mint ice cream."

I laughed because her eyes rolled back in her head when she mentioned the ice cream. "That sounds good to me too, but I want to work on my album for a few hours first."

"Alright y'all, are you ready to hear the debut of Ms. Elle Jamison?" DJ Spin announced.

"Yessssssssss!" the crowd yelled.

"Elle, we got over here just in time! Look who I found in the crowd! Savior invited her and made sure she got here for your big moment!" Pepper stated as she and Saveon walked over with someone trailing behind him.

As soon as he moved, my mouth dropped open. "Mama! I can't believe you came!"

"Baby, I don't care how much we fight, I would never miss out on you singing! Elle, I'm sorry for taking GT's side over yours. I only wanted you to have a better life than I had. When you broke off your engagement, it gave me time to think about how I had treated you. I was wrong to take their side over yours, Elle. I'm proud of you for finally breaking free and going after your dreams. I love you, baby. Can you forgive me?"

Wrapping my arms around my mama, I answered, "Yes, I forgive you, Mama. You just have to let me live my life the way I want to."

"I hear you, baby. I remember when you used to belt out songs all over the house. Now, look at you! You just signed your first record deal, and all these people are about to hear you sing!"

I laughed because she used to joke about me screeching through the house. But even with me getting on her nerves, she worked overtime to make sure I had voice and dance lessons every week. "Thank you, Mama, for making sure I was able to take classes to follow my dreams. Tonight, all those hours of classes and you working overtime are paying off."

"Okay, y'all, it's about to start. Saveon, help Miyanda up, so we can go to the railing and watch everyone's reaction to Elle's debut," Pepper directed.

The five of us walked over as Saveon's last snippet played. I was a ball of nerves because I knew my song was next. As the music changed, my voice filled the air. Just like Savior said, I watched the crowd as they slow danced, swayed, and got into my song. Judging by the looks and smiles on their faces, they loved it.

Tears fell from my eyes as my song ended, and everyone stood up and clapped. All I could do was wave and thank every-one. My mama had tears streaming down her face and for the first time in years, I could see genuine pride in her eyes. "You did it, baby! That was beautiful, and the crowd loved it! I can't wait to hear the rest of that song and your album."

"Hey, baby. Surprise!" I heard from behind me.

My head snapped around, and Grant was standing there with Brooke and Raven. My whole mood dropped and I wondered how the hell he got in. "Why are you here, Grant? I told you before that we are finished. If you are here to start some shit, please leave."

"I just came to see if you were really hoeing yourself out for a contract. Judging by the announcement, I see that you aren't who I thought you were."

Saveon stepped in front of me and threatened, "Watch your mouth, before I knock your punk ass out!"

"You don't scare me, choir boy! That's my bitch, and I will talk to her any fucking way I feel like! You and your brother think the sun rises and sets on your ass, but I will lay both you mutherfuckers out!"

Pepper and I exchanged looks, then she ran off, and I knew she was going to get Savior.

"GT, fuck this sorry hoe! This bitch ain't even worthy of being a Wells!" Brooke spat.

"You need to shut the fuck up, Brooke! The only hoe here is you and that skank beside you!" Miyanda yelled.

Turning to Miyanda, I said, "No, please don't get yourself upset. I don't want you hurting yourself or the baby. I'm not worried about Brooke because she's just bitter and evil."

"Miyanda, you better be glad your ass is pregnant! Don't be mad at me because your man left you for a real woman! Elle, don't fuck around and get your ass whooped at your own party! You know how I give it!"

Walking to Brooke, I looked her dead in the face and said, "I've taken your shit for years, off the strength of our fucked-up friendship! But that shit is dead, and I will lay your fake ass out if you keep trying me!"

She tried to step to me but was yanked back by security. Savior walked up with Matese, Doom, and Jace in tow. "Saveon, bruh, step back and let me handle this mutherfucker. Matese, get these bitches out of here! Elle, don't even worry about these jealous ass hoes! Grant, stay the fuck away from Elle before I forget who I am and revert back to the monster I used to be."

The paparazzi flooded our section, and security was overrun, trying to get them out.

Raven grabbed one of the reporters, and they started videotaping as she ran back over and screamed, "I'm not going anywhere until the whole world hears the truth about this bitch! GT has always been in love with me, but you trapped him by getting pregnant, so he stayed with you! Well, we are engaged now, and I no longer have to hide the fact that GT is the father of my two kids! So, you and your dead baby need to leave us the fuck alone!"

I snapped and started beating Raven's ass! My fists were doing all the talking after she mentioned me losing my baby. A strong pair of arms pulled me off her and whispered in my ear before Grant let me go.

"I'm sorry, Elle, she doesn't mean anything to me. I love you!"

"Mutherfucker, get your hands off her! Tese, get Elle out of here!" I heard Savior yell, before he grabbed Grant and punched him in the mouth.

All hell had broken loose around me, and I was looking for Miyanda and my mama. Before I could take a step, Matese grabbed me and rushed me through the melee of fights toward an unmarked door.

Once he opened it, there was a set of stairs leading to an outside door.

"Wait, we have to find my mama and Miyanda! Plus, we have to go back for Savior!"

Matese kept moving me down the steps and placed me in the back of the limo as he explained, "Saveon, Doom, and Jace grabbed your mama along with the other ladies and took them out right before the fight broke out. They should be headed back to the villas now. Vern is up there with Savior, and I know they should be down here soon. Just relax and have a drink, Tyson."

After he closed the car door and went to his spot up front, I stared out the window looking for Savior. As I waited, my mind went through what just happened upstairs. It hit me that Grant had two babies on me. Raven and I were pregnant at the same time, and her baby was born a month before I was supposed to have Ivy. While I was trying to salvage our relationship, this man had a whole fucking hidden family!

No matter how much I tried to hold them in, the tears came streaming down my face. I had given Grant so much of me, and he took it and gave it to another woman. Shaking my head, I grabbed the bottle of Hennessey, removed the bow, then poured the glass to the top.

I downed most of it and let the liquid burn in my throat. It helped to ease the pain that was in my heart that Grant caused. Every time I thought about his raw dicking ass, I gulped more.

The door opened, and Savior got in. His clothes were messed up and his hands were bleeding, but other than that, he looked fine. He eyed the glass in my hand, then took it from me and downed the rest of the liquid that was inside of it.

"Sorry about that but beating GT's ass made me thirsty as hell. Do you want another glass?"

"Yeah, here."

I handed him the bottle, and he filled two glasses to the top. Savior tapped on the window for the driver to go. We both sat and drank in silence, and he refilled once our cups were empty. The liquor was hitting me hard, but it was needed after the night I just had. It was still fucking with me about Grant having babies with Raven. She used to bring them to the studio, and I remembered oohing and ahhing over them. This bitch even let me hold one of her sons, while she recorded a fucking song! Knowing damn well he was my fiancé's son!

"I understand why you are upset, Elle. But after you get that shit out, don't waste another tear on GT's no-good ass! You deserve better than him, and that's why you made the choice to get out. I guarantee you right now he is somewhere fucking Raven while you are in here shedding tears."

"I know, it's just fucked up to realize that the person who was supposed to love you and take care of your heart is the same one who tears it apart. I just want someone to love me like I love them, Savior. Is that too much to ask?" I slurred.

"And that's what you should have, Elle. I mean, you are fine as hell and have a good heart. Any man would be happy to have you on their arm and in his bed."

The car suddenly stopped, and the window for the driver came down. Matese looked at us and said, "He's dropping me off. Are you sure you don't want me to stay with y'all tonight at the studio? Maybe you all need to stay here at the villa, cause that bottle of Hennessey is almost gone."

"Naw man, we are cool. We are just going to lay some of these emotions down on a track. You head on, bruh, me and Elle are good."

"Alright then, Jace left you something in the door. See you both tomorrow," Tese stated, then he left.

The limo took off as Savior pulled out a blunt and lit it, passing it to me. As soon as I inhaled, I sat back and watched him refill our glasses.

"Pepper is going to be pissed we finished off this bottle in one night. I don't know why, but this shit is hitting me harder than usual. Are you hot?" Savior asked.

Nodding my head, I drank most of my glass then put it down. I kicked my heels off and responded, "It's hot as hell in here. Let down the window."

He opened the windows and the sunroof above. I moved over to the seat beside him, so I could be under the sunroof to feel the breeze. We smoked and drank in silence for a minute, as the limo headed toward the studio that was forty-five minutes away from the villas.

I was finally relaxed, and my body felt different. Brown liquor was never my thing, but I was thankful for it tonight.

"I see you finally took your ring off. What was it two or three carats?"

"Grant said it was three carats. He bought it for me after he got served for a paternity suit. I didn't even like it, but I didn't say shit because I loved him. Hell, I wasn't even going to get my wedding the way I wanted with him."

"That's fucked up! I got Lake a ten-carat ring, and I was going to give her a big ass wedding, but she just wanted something small."

"I wanted a wedding with just us, you know. With red roses everywhere and me in a long, slinky Grecian goddess dress. But Grant wanted a gawdy ass bedazzled wedding! Fuck his cheating ass! Do you know he hasn't fucked me in over six months? I have needs, but he's been too busy slinging dick to everyone else to care!"

Savior shook his head, then pulled his shirt off and slurred, "He's a stupid mutherfucker! If you were mine, I would be fucking you every time my dick twitched. Then, I would suck on your pussy until your shit ran dry!"

My pussy throbbed at his words and sight of his naked torso. His muscles bulged and his body had several tattoos. The one that stood out the most, was a beautiful cross with names on it. I couldn't help but touch it as the red roses intertwined with it. I traced the outline of it and then the names.

"This is beautiful, Savior."

"Yeah, I had it done after my parents and my little sister, Faith, were killed in a car accident. When Lake and my child were murdered, I added their names. I named our baby, Angel because I never got to hold her because I was in a coma when they were buried. We had just gotten married and was celebrating starting a new life together. Having everyone you love stripped away from you, takes a piece of your soul, Elle. Especially when you are the reason your soul mate and child are dead."

Moving into his lap, I held his face in my hands, leaned in, and kissed his lips softly. At first, he didn't return the kiss. Then, Savior grabbed me, deepened the kiss, and we started going at each other.

My body was on fire, and I was horny as hell! The combination of the weed and Hennessey, had me ready for anything. Breaking the kiss between us, I raised up and took my dress off and was naked except for my thong.

"Damn, you are beautiful, Elle. Are you sure you want to do this? We are both drunk and high as fuck! I don't want you to regret this in the morning. Please tell me now because my dick is hard as hell, and once we start, I'm going to fuck the shit out of you in this limo."

My answer was to drop to my knees. I pulled his thick chocolate dick out, and started licking the tip, then sucked as much of him in as I could.

Savior grabbed my hair and started slowly pumping into my mouth. "Mmmm, suck that shit, Elle!"

I coated his dick in saliva and hummed as I suctioned all the precum from the tip. The more he moaned, the wetter my pussy got. It had never gotten this wet from sucking dick before.

Pulling his dick from my mouth, I grabbed the glass of Hennessey and dipped his balls in the liquid. "What you about to do, Elle, turn a nigga out?"

"Just sit back and let me do my thing"

He smiled and slurred, "I love that freaky shit! As long as you don't touch my ass, I'm down for whatever!'

I laughed and sat the glass back down on the console. His balls and the bottom part of his dick was dripping in Hennessey. Starting with his balls, I lifted them and sucked them, enjoying the taste of Savior and liquor until there was no more left. I swirled my tongue around his shaft, sucking and licking until he growled and yanked me up by my hair.

"Fuck that! You not about to make a mutherfucker crazy over your freaky ass! Stick your head out the sunroof and don't move!"

I stood up and put my head out the sunroof. The lights of the city shone bright, and the warm desert air cooled off the sweat on my body. I felt so free and didn't even care if my breast were exposed.

A pair of hands parted my legs below, and I felt Savior part my pussy and run his big fingers up and down the slit. His thumb massaged my clit, and my legs got weak as my pussy contracted and begged for relief.

When I felt his tongue and mouth latch on to my sensitive clit, my knees buckled, and I screamed out into the night. "Savior, damn!"

"Yeah, let them know who's eating the fuck out of your pussy!"

Savior got on his knees and put my legs on his shoulders with his face, facing my treasure. Resting on his shoulders, he stuck his tongue into my walls as he massaged my clit with his fingers. As the pressure built, I pinched my nipples and started riding Savior's tongue as he caressed my spot with precision.

When my orgasm hit me, I squirted all over Savior's face and screamed into the air. Savior placed me on the limo seat, placed my legs on his shoulders, and scooted my butt to the edge of the seat. My pussy was still dripping, but I was still horny as hell! It was hot and both of us were sweating and panting. But it didn't stop him from lining his long dick up with my opening and pushing inside of me.

When he started stroking, it started off slow and deliberate. He bent down and sucked my titty and nipped at my nipple, causing me to moan and squirm in his arms. I reached down and squeezed his balls as Savior stroked me deeply.

"Baby, I'm about to cum all in this good ass pussy! You gonna have my baby, Lake?" Savior slurred as he picked up speed.

I frowned because he thought I was his wife. Savior and I were both intoxicated, but this felt strange. I tried to push him away, but it felt so good, and my orgasm was so close. My head started spinning, and I felt myself getting dizzy as my pussy clenched and sent me spiraling into another mind-blowing orgasm.

Savior pushed my legs back to my head and started fucking me fast and deeply. I felt the pressure building again, and I grabbed his ass and started pushing him deeper into me, as I threw my pussy back on him.

"Fuck!!!!!!!!!!! I love you, Lake!" he growled as he fucked me so hard, my teeth hurt. Then with one final push, he dumped so much nut in me, I felt him pulsing as it streamed out of his dick.

"Yes!" I screamed as my third orgasm hit me, and he grinded into my clit, making me cream all over him.

Savior kissed me, and his tongue made love to mine in the aftermath. He pulled back and his face was different. Like he was sleepwalking or high on something. I was barely hanging on and felt myself fading as his speech slurred, while he continued calling me Lake. His dick grew hard inside of me again, and he started stroking my sore pussy back to life.

He used his thumb and finger to pinch my clit as he pounded into me. My body craved his touch and was searching for more of the pleasure Savior had given me. When he eased his finger in my ass, I came hard and saw black spots invade my vision.

Savior nutted in me again and finally, collapsed on top of me. The last thing I remembered before my world went black was his dick growing harder again inside of me.

I was beyond pissed off because I had been waiting for Savior to come back to his villa ever since I left the party. Two hours ago, he came back with that bitch, Elle, and they had been fucking ever since!

That was my drugged dick she was riding like a happy hoe! They had finally stopped fucking about an hour ago, and I was waiting outside the bedroom window, to sneak in and steal the condom, so I could get pregnant that way.

My phone buzzed, and I saw it was Brooke finally calling me back. Answering, I whispered, "Where the fuck have you been, Brooke? You were supposed to help me with Savior!"

"I had other shit I had to work on, Kiara! You act like I didn't put the drugged Hennessey inside of Savior's limo. All you had to do was wait for him to get to the villa, right?"

Sighing in frustration, I replied, "No, he came back with Elle, and they have been fucking the hell out of each other all night! I thought GT said she wasn't a hoe and would only fuck him? Because she sure has been riding Savior's dick like it's hers!"

"Wait, you mean Elle fucked Savior! Damn, I didn't know the heifer really had it in her! Are they still in there fucking? Because that bottle had a lot of shit in it, and I'm sure that dick is fire! Ooh, maybe you can get them on video!"

"No, they finally fell out about an hour ago. I'm going to sneak in and see if I can't get one of the condoms and use it to inseminate myself. One way or the other, Savior is giving me a baby and bringing his ass back to me!"

"Listen, Looney Bitch, you do know that shit probably won't work right. Maybe you can fake a miscarriage and blame it on Savior. I mean, I can get someone to come and beat your ass and make it look good."

"No, Brooke, I want Savior back! Look, I need to go in there before the sun comes up. I'm just hoping they don't wake up until I get what I need."

"I doubt it! They are probably dead to the world! Even if Savior woke up and caught you, he probably wouldn't remember it. Elle doesn't drink brown liquor, so she probably is just tired from being fucked by that drugged out dick! You know, the dick you were supposed to be enjoying right now."

Brooke was cracking up, and it made me want to beat her ass! This shit wasn't a joke to me because Savior was my ticket to the next stage of stardom. Plus, I really had feelings for him and wanted us to be together.

"That's not funny, Brooke! Look, I'll call you back!"

Hanging up on her, I looked around, then opened the

window and crawled in. Once I was inside, Savior and Elle were on their backs in the bed knocked out. They were both naked and snoring, so I guess Brooke was right about them being dead to the world.

I looked into the trash cans in the bedroom and the bathroom. But there were no used condoms or wrappers. Stomping back into the room, I stared at Savior's dick, and my blood boiled. He had fucked this hoe raw! Never in the months when we were together had he been inside me without protection. His dick had dried cum all over it, and Elle's thighs had it too. I wanted to beat both of their nasty asses, but that wasn't going to help me get pregnant.

I sat down in the chair across from the bed to think. How the hell was I going to get Savior's seeds without a condom. The answer came to me, and I quickly took off my panties under my dress.

Slowly, I climbed on the bed and straddled his semi-hard dick. Moaning, I slid down on it and started riding it softly. It had been so long since I had my man's dick inside my pussy, that I came just from him being inside of me.

For the next twenty minutes, I rode his dick, but nothing was happening. If anything, he got soft inside of me, and I knew this bitch had milked him dry. Reaching over, I smacked the shit out of her, but the hoe didn't even move.

Another thought came to me, but I didn't know exactly how to do it. Getting off the bed, I went to the bathroom and grabbed one of the plastic cups. Standing over Elle, I pushed her legs apart, and looked into her pussy to see if there was some sperm left.

I saw mostly dried sperm and needed her to push some fresh wet sperm out for me. "Dammit, I don't want to touch this bitch, but I need these damn seeds!"

Chewing on my nail, I wondered if this shit was even worth it. Looking over at Savior, I knew it was. Getting back on the bed, I put the cup to Elle's pussy and started stroking her clit. If this heifer could cum, maybe she would push out some nut, and I could scoop it out and take a cup of it. The bitch moaned and opened her legs, calling Savior's name and grinding against my finger. After five minutes, this hoe still hadn't cum, and the sun was starting to creep up.

Rolling my eyes, I bent down and started licking and sucking on her pussy.

"Yes!" she moaned in her sleep and grabbed my hair and pushed me into her pussy.

Finally, her clit hardened, and the bitch started creaming everywhere. I pulled back and started scooping up anything coming out of her. Then, I scraped the remaining juices using the rim of the cup. I smiled because at least I wasn't leaving empty-handed!

Climbing off the bed, I was about to leave when something caught my attention. I crushed the cup in my hand as tears fell from my eyes. My first thought was to set them both on fire and watch them burn, but that would have been too easy. I wanted them to suffer.

Pulling out my phone in anger, I walked over to the bed and started snapping pictures of both of them naked. These photos will definitely be used in my plans. One last look at the bed, I headed out the window and walked over to my own villa.

Dialing Brooke's number, I put it on speaker and started packing my bags. I needed to move to another hotel in order to work on my new plan.

"Girl, I was about to go to bed, what the hell do you want now!"

Closing my suitcase, I responded, "Forget my plan, Brooke. I need your help with something else. You won't believe what I found out."

"Aw hell, what now?"

After I told Brooke what I found, she agreed to help me get my revenge. If Elle and Savior thought they were getting away with hurting me, they had another thing coming!

"Who was that, baby?"

"Kiara's crazy ass! But she did give me some information about Elle that we need to act on soon. I wish we could have gotten her ass on tape with Big Tex before Savior signed her."

My lover got up and stretched, drawing my attention to their body. I couldn't wait to work out this stress, I had built up.

"Yeah, this really fucks up our plans. We need to act fast, before your brother figures out that you've been embezzling money from him. All hell is going to break loose once GT realizes he's almost broke. But I can't lie and say his money doesn't look good in our offshore account, but we need more. People are getting suspicious and asking me for my accounting books. We need to move fast before we're caught by the authorities or the people we've scammed. I'm ready to pop some babies in your ass once we land in Belize. You are going to be one rich woman by the time we finish stealing this money. We just have to figure out how."

"I know bae, but my brother is so preoccupiedwith Elle dumping him. I have a plan that involves Elle. By the time I get finished with her, she will be our puppet and do anything we want. Which means getting us access to Savior Morrison's bank account. Kiara gave me her account number the other day, so we can clean out her stupid ass too! There are a few more of my clients I have lined up, to clean them out as well."

My baby came to me and kissed me with so much passion, my pussy throbbed. As soon as I laid back, my breast was sucked on, and I arched my back. I smiled, knowing this was going to be a long night.

"You are beautiful, smart, and devious as hell! That's why I love you, Brooke."

"I love you too, Doom."

The pounding on the door was what woke me up out of my sleep. My head felt heavy and it was throbbing. Not to mention, my mouth was super dry, and my body was sore as hell, especially my pussy.

The last thing I remember was being in the limo with Savior. Opening my eyes, I realized I wasn't in my room. There was an arm wrapped around my waist, and I was butt ass naked. Turning to the side, Savior was stirring in his sleep. I froze, remembering bits and pieces of last night. Flashes of me riding Savior's face hanging out of the sunroof made me embarrassed as hell! I needed to get the hell out of here before he woke up!

Before I could even move, Savior's eyes popped open. He frowned at me, then his eyes moved down my naked body and then snapped back to my face.

"Damn, I take it the Hennessey took over last night. I don't remember even coming back here. The last thing I remember, was eating your pussy last night. Are you alright?"

Nodding softly, I said, "Yeah, but my head is pounding and so is my body. I don't remember how we got back here either. But from what I see, we didn't use protection. I need to know when the last time was you were tested. I was a few days before coming to Vegas, and I'm clean, but I'm not on birth control, so I need to get a Plan B."

"Yeah, I was tested a few weeks ago, and I'm clean as well. We can get the butler to grab the Plan B for you. I'm just sorry I don't remember what happened because judging by how raw my dick feels and all those hickeys on your neck, breasts, and thighs, we must have had a good ass night!"

I smiled and replied, "Yeah, I wish I remembered too! I've never been so drunk that I can't remember things. Maybe it was the combination of the champagne, the weed, and Hennessey. Do you regret what happened between us?"

"Elle, there are a lot of things I regret in life, but this isn't one of them. We are both grown as hell and were attracted to each other, so it happened. I just don't want it to mess up our friendship and the vibe we have going on in the studio. Not to mention, you are just starting out, and I don't want people to think you slept your way into a contract. The last thing you need is the gossip blogs dragging your name. It's bad enough the rumors were going around about us before the announcement. Shit, Pepper is probably going to dig in our ass this morning about the fight at the party."

Moaning, I stated, "Ughhhhhh I forgot about that! Maybe if we—

Boom! Boom! Boom!

Savior stood up and explained, "Damn, it's one o'clock! No telling who that is at the door. Here's a robe to cover up with. Nine times out of ten, it's Matese, my brother, or Pepper."

After we both put on our robes, Savior went and answered the door, and I sat down on the couch in the living room area. Pepper and Saveon entered the room, and Pepper was so mad, she was turning red.

"Pepper, before you start going in on us, remember we tried not to fight those mutherfuckers, but they kept on fucking with us," Savior commented.

"Naw, bruh, let her pace for a minute cause y'all really got my baby stressed the hell out!" Saveon explained.

Savior came and sat down beside me on the couch. We both looked at each other, wondering what the hell was going on.

"Do you two know the shitstorm you have started? You let me go in front of the press last night and risk my reputation, by telling everyone you two weren't sleeping with each other. But judging by your actions, I can see that wasn't the whole truth."

I replied, "I'm sorry, Pepper. We really weren't messing with each other when you talked to the press. After the party last night, we drank the bottle of Hennessey you left and smoked some weed. One thing led to another in the limo and somehow, we woke up in bed together. If you are worried about us sleeping together getting out, we've already decided to remain friends."

"Elle is right. Hell, to be honest with you, neither one of us remembers what happened last night or how we got back here. The last thing we both remember is being in the limo. I'm going to have to ask Matese what kind of weed it was because you know I'm not a lightweight. Hopefully, that shit wasn't laced because it fucked both Elle and me up. That reminds me, I need to order some Tylenol and something else.

Saveon and Pepper looked at each other, then frowned.

"Wait, I didn't leave a bottle of Hennessey in the limo last night. I didn't have time because we had to switch drivers, remember. The only thing that was supposed to be in there was champagne, bottle water, coke, and ice. Saveon, call Matese."

"Way ahead of you, bae. I'm texting him to head over here now. Bruh, you two don't have any memories from last night?"

Savior looked at me, and we both shook our heads no.

I added, "Well, I remember a few things that happened in the limo, but I don't have a clue on how we got back here. What's going on?"

"Hold up, Pepper. If you didn't leave me the bottle of Hennessey, then who did?"

Pepper bit her lip and said, "I think you two were drugged. Because fucking wasn't the only thing you two were doing last night. Elle, look at your hand."

I frowned and raised my hands and gasped. Why the hell hadn't I noticed this shit when I woke up? On my left finger was the biggest ring I'd seen in my life. It was a vintage-looking, emerald cut diamond ring with diamonds surrounding it. The ring was at least fifteen carats and had a matching emerald cut band below it. Savior grabbed my hand, and he was just as shocked as I was. My eyes moved to his left hand, where a matching diamond band graced his finger too.

"What the hell is going on?" I asked as my voice trembled.

Pepper pulled out her phone and said, "Well, for one, Savior just dropped a cool three million on that rock on your finger, and this is just one of thousands of headlines of you two this morning. Your asses are splashed all over the TV, internet, and radio. There are paparazzi camping outside the villa gates, just waiting to get photos of the newly married couple."

She showed us pictures from Zee with the Tea, showing us at a wedding chapel getting married. We both looked high as hell, and we were all over each other. The headline read, *"GT Who?!"*

"Alright look, it was obvious we were drunk. All we have to do is get it annulled and then this shit will die down," Savior stated.

Pepper shook her head and responded, "No, you two can't get a quickie divorce! Your careers will both be tarnished! Kiara has already made you out to be some hoe-hopping, dick-showing, deadbeat dad, Savior. The last thing you need is a twenty-four-hour marriage. Not to mention, Elle just broke up with her fiancé who you were producing. Her singing career has barely started, and she's already been seen as a gold-digging hoe and fighter. The silver lining is what Raven announced last night. She told the world that GT had two babies on you, Elle. So, those two are getting dragged as well in the press. We can use that to our advantage to get ahead of this mess, by spinning the two of you in this whirlwind romance. People love a love story, and we are going to give them just that. Two broken hearts, finding each other in the studio. Now, I say you need to stay married for at least six months. Then you two can get a divorce, and people will just say it didn't work out. Now that solves one problem, but then we need to figure out who drugged you two."

"I don't even know what to say about this shit. But why do I have a feeling this shit has Kiara written all over it," Savior added.

"I was thinking the same thing, bruh, but GT could also have something to do with it too. Matese said he will be here in about twenty minutes. Maybe you two need to both get dressed, so we can figure this shit out," Saveon added.

Nodding, I stood up and said, "I need to go over to my villa, so I can get some clean clothes. I'll shower there and be back here in ten minutes."

Pepper added, "Your mama is there. We figured you wouldn't mind, so we brought her here after the party. After breakfast, she said she was about to take a nap. Just a heads-up, she's not happy she wasn't invited to your wedding. I'm going to set up an interview with a friend of mine for later this afternoon. You two will have to get your story straight. So, let's all meet back here in about an hour."

"Thanks, Pepper. Let me go over here and talk to her and explain what happened. Then, I will be back."

"Do you need me to walk you over there?" Savior asked as he stood up and walked me to the door.

"No, I need a minute to process all of this. Do you want me to help pay for the ring? I'm sure it cost more than I make in several lifetimes, so it might have to be in a few payments."

He lifted his hand and rubbed my face. "I have plenty of money, Elle. Whatever it cost, it's a gift, and I want you to keep it. Plus, it looks good on your hand. We don't have to talk about the marriage now, but I will look into other ways to get out of it, Elle. The last thing I wanted was to put you in a bad situation, when your singing career is just beginning."

A wave of sadness hit me as he looked desperate to get out of our marriage. I shook it off though because what Savior and I shared, was meant for only one night. Neither of us asked to be drugged.

"Whatever you and Pepper think is best. I will see you in a few minutes, Savior."

As I walked over to the villa I was renting, my mind was going a mile a minute. Who drugged us and why? What the hell was I going to do about being married to Savior?

MATESE

"Vern, make sure everyone is at their assigned spots. We have paparazzi at the gates, and you know they will do anything to get a picture, so be on the lookout. I also sent pictures to everyone's messenger of who is not allowed in this area. Pepper contacted the police to help us with crowd control. When they get here, you can just send them to my villa, and I'll give them directions."

"Okay, boss. I'm about to have them do sweeps every ten minutes instead of every twenty."

Nodding my head, I answered, "Sounds like a plan. Hit me up if you have any questions."

Once he nodded, I headed toward my villa. Pulling out my phone, I dialed Ross's number.

"What's up, Tese?"

"Hey, Ross, have you heard anything about Yo yet?"

"Naw, that mutherfucker got ghost. Blast and I have our crew sitting on his people's houses, but nothing yet."

Running a hand down my face in frustration, I replied, "Fuck! I know Yo, and he's up to something. I just wish I knew what it was."

"Tese, I know you have a whole crew of bodyguards out there, but they are clean. For all we know, Yo could be on his way out to Vegas to do some shit. I don't play about my fam, so I'm headed your way tonight. Blast can take care of shit here."

"Not going to lie and say I wouldn't mind having you at my back. Saveon, Savior, Doom, and Jace are here. But you know the Morrison Brothers are in the spotlight, so they can't get dirty. But won't your boyfriend and girlfriend be pissed off about you flying off to Vegas? I mean, you can bring them too if you want."

"Naw, I caught Orlando cheating on me, and Amber's ass is getting too clingy. I'm single as fuck! I'm ready to find someone to settle down with and have some kids. I want what you and Catrina have."

Him mentioning Catrina, had me thinking about the fucked-up situation I was in. Last night had been nice going out to the party together. All the shit with Janiyah wasn't there, and Catrina opened back up to me. Before all the shit went down, we danced and had fun like we used to. Once I got back to the villa, we made love, and it was the best feeling in the world. Just as I was about to go for round two, we got a call from Mashelle saying Janiyah needed a doctor. Once the doctor came, Trina assisted him, and Janiyah grabbed my hand while he examined her.

I was stuck on what to do, but Catrina nodded for me to continue, and I held Janiyah's hand until she fell asleep. Once we left Mashelle's villa where Janiyah was staying, Trina she shut back down again and wouldn't say a word to me.

"Ross, she's not feeling me right now. Especially not with Janiyah being here. But look, head on here so you can meet your godson, Maurice."

"That's what's up! Let me get shit straight here, and I'm on my way. Tese, you are going to have to decide soon, because it's not fair having them both in limbo."

"I hear you, Ross. See you when you get here."

After hanging up, I put the phone in my pocket and headed toward my villa. Passing by Mashelle's, I saw Janiyah out on the patio crying. Rushing over to her, I asked, "Janiyah, what's wrong. Are you in pain? Do you need me to call the doctor again?"

"No, I'm not in pain. It just hit me that I won't be alive to see Yolanda get married or Maurice have his first child. When I die, Maurice will at least have you, Matese. But what about my daughter? Yo and his family are evil, and I don't want her to grow up with them. It's no telling how she will turn out."

Sitting down beside her, I grabbed her hand and said, "Janiyah, stop talking like you aren't going to be here. Alexis and Catrina are working overtime to find a study to get you in. You will be here to raise both of your children. I also would never leave Maurice's sister to be raised or mistreated by Yo. But Niyah, you have to stop this crying shit and fight! This isn't the Niyah that I loved! You always were strong and didn't let anything get you down."

"I'm just tired, Matese. Everyday is nothing but pain and weakness! Don't you think I want to fight? I'm not the same

Janiyah you fell in love with! She's gone just like the love you used to have for me! You love Catrina, and I don't blame you because she's better than me! Smart, beautiful, and one of the nicest people I have ever known. That's why I know my kids would be better off with me dead because they would have you two."

That shit pissed me off, and I yanked Janiyah's ass up. Pushing her against the bannister, on the pergola, I grabbed her by the throat and growled, "Don't say shit like that ever again, Niyah! You act like your kids and I wouldn't be fucked up if you left this earth today! No one could replace you, so stop fucking acting like your life doesn't matter!"

She stared into my eyes, with tears falling from hers. All the memories of what we had, flooded through me as I stared into the face of the woman who was supposed to be my wife. The thought of her dying was killing me, and to hear her giving up made it worse.

Without thinking, I growled and kissed Janiyah. My dick bricked up when she jumped up and wrapped her arms and legs around me. I felt the heat from her pussy through the thin basketball shorts I had on. She started grinding on me, and I cupped her ass and pressed her into me. Reaching under her dress, I tore the thong away as I nibbled on her neck. She reached into my shorts and pulled my dick out.

When Janiyah put it near her opening and rubbed my head in her juices, I plunged in, causing us both to moan.

We started fucking the shit out of each other and all the pent-up feelings and frustrations, were being taken out of me with each stroke. Our tongues were battling with each other as

Janiyah's walls clenched around my dick. She screamed my name as her orgasm hit, and her shit started milking the nut out of my dick as I exploded inside of her.

I pulled away from her mouth as her pussy throbbed around my dick, and it instantly hardened. She started riding it slowly again, and I moaned. We stared at each other, panting as the pleasure rose up in us again. I watched her eyes roll back, and her mouth open wide as another orgasm hit her. My own came straight from my nut and surged through my dick. I slammed into her over and over again, dumping ropes of seeds into her womb.

This time her legs dropped, and we held each other. Once we pulled away, I instantly felt like shit. What the fuck had I done?

"Well, I guess you made your choice, seeing as how you just fucked her right across from where you made love to me at last night. Since I don't see a condom on, I guess, I see how much you care about my health and the health of our baby," Catrina stated.

Whipping around, I saw Catrina standing there with tears streaming down her reddened face. Mashelle looked at me with disgust and said, "Put your fucking dick up, Tese! You are foul as fuck! Bitch, you better be glad you are already half-dead, so I won't beat your ass right now! But you have to find somewhere else to stay! I don't allow homewrecking hoes where my man lays his head!"

Janiyah stepped forward after pulling her dress down and said, "Catrina, I'm so sorry! It's my fault not Matese's. I came on to him."

"You don't have to lie, Janiyah. I was sitting on the edge of our pool with my feet in, so I heard and saw it all. I watched as the man I loved, grabbed another woman, and fucked her with passion! Then dropped the kids that were meant to be mine inside of her, not once but twice! So, you can save your lies and congratulations on getting your man back! It's okay though, Mashelle. She can have the villa with her man. Me and my child are going back to Nashville," Catrina stated, before turning around and walking back to the villa.

I pushed my dick in my shortss and ran over to Catrina, grabbing her before she could get inside. "Baby, please don't do this! It was a mistake! I love you and our baby, Trina! Don't give up on us, please!"

"Matese, I wasn't the one who have up on us, you did! I told you before that I would never play second fiddle to any woman, and I won't. I'll let you know when I deliver. You won't have to worry about me being a bitter baby mama either. Once he or she is born, you can see them anytime you want. Goodbye, Matese."

"Excuse me, I'm looking for Matese Reyes!" a police officer yelled, walking into the yard with five others.

"I'm Matese, but just give me a minute, and I will let you know where you all can assist the rest of the guards."

"Sir, I'm not here for that. Please, place your hands behind your back!" he ordered.

Mashelle and Janiyah both walked over, and Catrina looked on in fear. I knew to cooperate because they would kill all our asses, and I didn't want the women I love to get hurt or see me die. So, I did as he said, and he cuffed me.

He turned to the women and said, "Are one of you ladies, Janiyah Hughes?"

"I'm Janiyah Hughes."

"Officer Williams, handcuff her too," the officer ordered.

"Ma'am, you are under arrest for the attempted murder of Yo' Anthony Davis. Williams, read Ms. Hughes her rights.

"Don't say shit, Janiyah, until the attorney gets there."

She nodded and looked down as they read her rights and took her out of the yard.

"Mr. Matese Reyes, you are under arrest for murder, you have—" the officer started but was interrupted.

"Wait, what the hell are you talking about? My brother hasn't murdered anyone!" Mashelle interrupted.

"I'm calling Onya and seeing if she can recommend a lawyer here, then I'm calling Savior! This is some bullshit!" Catrina stated as she got on her phone.

Mashelle was going off and the last thing I needed was for her to get arrested. Especially, when I knew she was about to hear some shit that might turn my sister against me.

So, I reluctantly said, "Shelle, I need you to take care of Trina and the kids for me. No matter what, remember I love you and have only tried to protect you. You know me, sis!"

"Of course, I'll take care of them. We are going to get you out of there, Tese. You know, I will bail you out as soon as you are arraigned."

"As I was saying, Matese Reyes. You are under arrest for the murder of Mario Reyes."

The officer read me my rights, but I was focused on my

sister's face. I saw disbelief, anger, and disappointment in her eyes. Mashelle started crying, and it made me feel like shit.

Right before they took me out, Mashelle stepped in front of me and asked the question, I had been dreading for years.

"Please tell me they have this shit wrong. There's no way you would do this to me! Stop looking like that and tell me the truth! Did you kill our father, Matese?"

"Damn, bruh, I can't believe you got married last night."

Saveon had stayed behind, while Pepper set up the interview for Elle and me. After taking a shower and ordering some breakfast, I finally was able to sit down and talk about the shit that was going on in my life.

Shaking my head, I responded, "Shit, I can't either, Saveon! I don't know what the fuck was in that bottle, but I don't remember anything past Elle and I doing some things in the limo. After that, I can't remember shit. I swear when I find out who did this shit to us, I'm beating their ass!"

"My bet is on your crazy ass ex! I told you something was wrong with her simple ass. But naw, you were trying to turn a dumb hoe into a smart one."

I laughed and responded, "Yeah, I fucked up. I can admit that shit now, but back then I was just trying to prove a point. You know, I never wanted to get married again after what happened to Lake. Especially, not to someone I'm working with. In the span of hours, I've broken every rule I've set for myself."

"Well at least it's Elle and not Kiara. If I had to pick a wife for you, she would be it, Save. She's beautiful, sweet, and will treat you right. We all know she's not after you for your money or fame, because although she doesn't make as much as you, Elle makes enough to be straight without you. That's probably a good thing since you both didn't sign a prenup."

"Fuck, that reminds me. I need to get the butler to get us some Plan B. Because of that drugged up ass bottle, it's no telling how many seeds I dropped in Elle last night. She already told me she's not on birth control. The last thing we need is a baby right now, when we are getting a divorce in six months," I stated, then texted the butler.

Saveon laughed and responded, "Shiiiiiiitttttttttt, you better let those seeds plant! At least with Elle, you would have a stable baby mama, instead of the rest of the skanks you've been running up in. You said you wanted kids, so that's a way to have one without the complications."

"Man, see, you are talking crazy! If I wanted to have kids, all I have to do is head over to your house and play with my nieces and nephews to get my fix. Plus, Elle just lost a child and I'm not sure she is ready for a baby. She barely broke up with her fiancé and now, she's stuck in a drunken marriage that neither one of us asked for."

"I'm sure you don't want to hear this, Save, but God works in mysterious ways. Maybe you two should give a relationship a try. We both know you two are attracted to each other. Before the drugs took over, you two were already freaking each other up. You both vibe with each other and are friends. The best relationships start off as friendship; look at Pepper and me."

"I don't know, Saveon. I'm still fucked up behind losing Lake. The last thing I want to do is hurt Elle because I haven't completely healed. That's not fair to her, especially with all the shit she has been through with GT."

"Man, I can't believe he had two babies on her. I knew he wasn't shit, but that takes the cake! You should have let me beat his ass last night. It's been a minute since I knocked somebody out!"

Laughing, I commented, "Naw, I handled him. He's been getting away with shit for too long now."

"You know Lake would want you to move on and be happy, right. She wouldn't want you being afraid to love another woman."

"I know that, but it still doesn't make it easy. For now, I just need to focus on Elle's career and making sure she's straight."

"Aw, look at you helping your wife shine! That's what's up, Save, make sure Mrs. Elle Morrison is made into the star she is supposed to be!"

Something about my brother saying Elle Morrison, felt right. But I didn't know how to feel about that feeling. Like Elle said earlier, I remembered bits and pieces of last night like the taste of Elle's sweet pussy, and the way she damn near snatched my soul when she went down on me. I also remembered being inside of her and feeling like it was home.

"Savior! You need to look at this shit now! I'm going to beat this bitch's ass if Elle doesn't get to her first!" Pepper yelled as she stormed into the villa.

Saveon stood up and wrapped his arms around her to calm her down. "Baby, you hardly ever cuss, what has Kiara done now."

She turned on the TV, and Kiara's face was on the screen as she was being interviewed by a reporter. Her right eye was black and swollen shut. There were bruises around Kiara's neck, and she was crying. It looked as if she was in a hospital bed, and the look on her face let me know Kiara was full of shit!

A sinking feeling went over me as she spoke.

"Hello everyone, this is Zee Fryer, and I am here with an exclusive interview with Kiara. I see that you are in a lot of pain. Tell us and our viewers what happened to you."

"Thank you, Zee for allowing me to tell my story. If I can, I want to be an example to other women who might be going through the same thing I am. No woman deserves to be hurt by the man they love."

"Are you telling us that Savior Morrison beat you?"

"Yes, he did this to me when I confronted him last night, after he married that homewrecking bitch, Elle! He beat me so bad, that I lost our baby this morning."

"Aw, hell naw! I'm calling Kut and putting this bitch on her radar! Pepper, give me my phone!" Saveon yelled.

I stood there, feeling a rage I had never felt before toward a woman. Never in my life have I wanted to put my hands on a woman, but Kiara was going to make me choke the shit out of her. My fist clenched because I knew this bitch was about to make me kill her. But I was in no way prepared for what Kiara had in store for me.

"I'm so sorry for your loss, Kiara. Savior Morrison needs to pay for what he's done. You need to go to police," Zee stated.

"I'm scared of what he will do to me. You have no idea what he's capable of or the vilest thing he did to me last night."

"Oh my God, what did he do to you that could be worse than losing your child?"

"Savior and his wife, Elle, raped me!"

I HAD JUST STEPPED OUT OF THE SHOWER AND SO MANY things was running through my mind. As I finished moisturizing my body, I looked at the huge rock on my finger. I still couldn't believe that I was Mrs. Savior Morrison. Everything from last night was still foggy, except those bits and pieces of us having sex. My pussy was sore and swollen from whatever else happened between us last night.

My feelings were all over the place when it came to Savior. I couldn't help but be attracted to not only his looks but his personality. Over the past few days, we've had some of the deepest and cleansing conversations that I'd had in a long time. Our losses bonded us in a way we never knew they would. We spent hours in the studio pouring that pain into the lyrics and making songs that spoke about love and passion.

The problem was we both had so much baggage. Kiara, for one, I could tell was going to be a problem. Not to mention, Savior wasn't over the death of his wife. If I was being honest, he might never be over it. At least not in a way that helped him move on. Savior proved that when he made it clear, he was looking for a way out.

On the flipside, I just broke my engagement with Grant and wasn't looking for another relationship this soon. Despite all the years of pain, I still loved Grant. I just wasn't in love with him anymore. It killed me finding out that he and Raven had two children while we were together. While I was mourning our daughter, he was more than likely holding his newborn son. How could I put my trust in another man, after all the shit I have been through? Grant used to be nice too but look how he ended up.

No, I was going to focus on this album and get through these six months of marriage to Savior. We were friends and like we agreed, I didn't want to lose that.

After I got dressed, I looked in the mirror and saw the myriad of hickeys on my neck and chest. I hoped Pepper had a makeup artist to cover all of them up. The black and purple Nike tights and matching sports bra would have to do until Miyanda got here to pick out what I was wearing for the interview.

I still needed to talk to my mama, but she was still sleeping. The one silver lining about last night, was my mama and I making up. Despite our disagreements, I loved her, and she had always been a good mother to me. Her sacrifices are what helped me be the woman, singer, and dancer I was today. I'm just hoping she wouldn't start asking Savior for stuff like she did Grant.

Grabbing my cell phone from the counter, I stepped out of

the bathroom door and felt something hard hit me in the back of the head. I fell face first onto the floor as pain exploded in my head. There was blood running in my face and eyes. Nausea and dizziness hit me hard, and I knew I had to have a concussion.

I tried to get up, but whoever hit me started beating me. The only thing I could do was ball up and protect my head. Pain was exploding throughout my body with each blow. I felt myself losing consciousness, and I knew whoever was doing this was going to kill me.

"Get off my baby!" I heard my mother scream.

The beating stopped, and I heard stuff breaking and my mama screaming. I was trying to fight through the pain and haze that was weighing me down, but it was too much. Something landed beside me, and I heard footsteps running.

Struggling, I opened my eyes and stared into the brown eyes that used to look at me with love, anger, and last night with pride. But now, they were blank and lifeless. She had given her life to save mine.

Inching toward my mama, I grabbed her hand and prepared to join her in the afterlife as I passed out.

To be continued in Part 2 the finale!

AUTHOR'S NOTE

Hey Boos! I am typing as fast as I can lol. But I've been slowed down since Covid. As most of you know, my son has special needs so between home-schooling and therapies its slowed the amount of writing I can do. Just hang in there with me because I have plenty coming! Part 2, Shifters PD, An Urban Fairytale Paranormal book, and sooooooo much more! I love you all! PLEASE LEAVE A REVIEW!!

ANNITIA L. JACKSON
PRESENTS

LOVE
IN THE LYRICS
FALLING FOR A MUSIC MOGUL
2

NATIONAL BESTSELLING AUTHOR
ANNITIA L. JACKSON

Coming soon the finale!

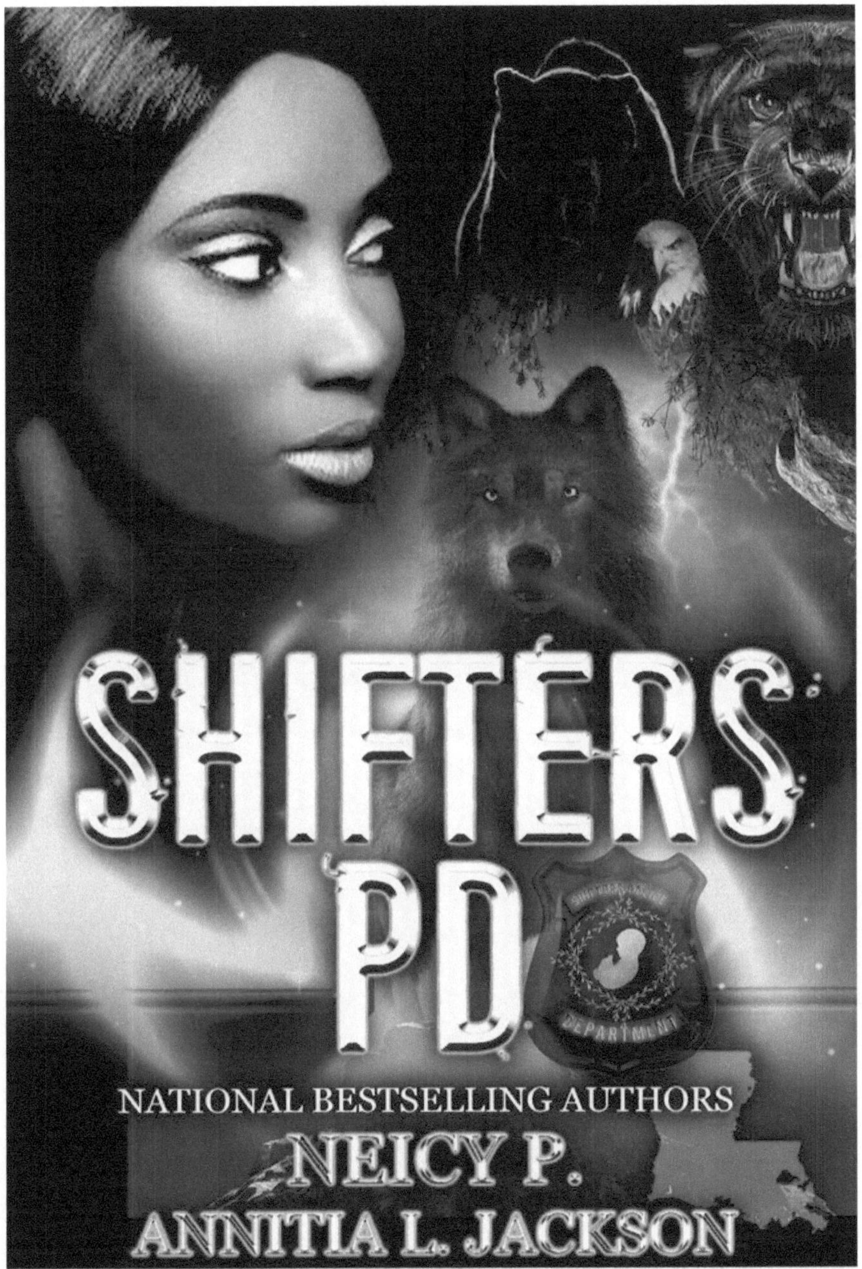
SHIFTERS PD
NATIONAL BESTSELLING AUTHORS
NEICY P.
ANNITIA L. JACKSON

ABOUT THE AUTHOR

This is book twenty-nine for me, and I'm excited to be able to share my work and creativity with all my old and new readers. As a new author in this literary world, I'm encouraged by your reviews and your willingness to read and hopefully enjoy my work. If you would like to join my reading

group, I am on Facebook and the name of the
group is Annitia's A-1 Readers Group.

ALSO BY ANNITIA L. JACKSON

Please check out my other titles listed on Amazon and Barnes & Noble:

D-City Chronicles Book One: Aja and Ro

D-City Chronicles Book Two: Aja and Ro

D-City Chronicles: The Finale

The Trinity Girl Chronicles: The Awakening

An Urban Christmas Story: Ebb and Bobbi

D-City Underworld: Zontae's Reign

D-City Underworld 2: Zontae's Reign

Loving a Heartless Queen

D-City Underworld 3: The Finale

Picking Up the Pieces of Her Shattered Soul

D-City Hit Squad: The Final Ride (Novella)

The Grass Ain't Always Greener (Anthology)

Kings of the Underworld: Alpha & Omega

Secret Seductions of an Incubus: A Paranormal Erotica Novella

A Fetish for Fur: A Holiday Paranormal Erotic Novella

From Savage to Saved: An Urban Christian Holiday Story

I Dare You to Love Me: A Complicated Love Story Novella

An Urban Valentine's Story: Ebb and Bobbi Novella

Best Friends with Twice the Benefits: An Erotica Novella

Kings of the Underworld Monroe: Rise of the Phoenix King

Bayou: King of the Rising Tides

Bayou 2: King of the Rising Tides

A Kut Above the Rest: Lovin' A Female Boss

A Kut Above the Rest 2: Lovin' A Female Boss

A Kut Above the Rest 3: Lovin' A Female Boss

Cupid Nights: A Shifter's PD Prequel (Collab)

A Touch of Death: Marci & Grave Novella

Just A Little Bit of Hope